THE CASTLE OF THE CARPATHIANS

Jules Verne

CONTENTS

THE CASTLE OF THE CARPATHIANS.1

CHAPTER I

This story is not fantastic; it is merely romantic. Are we to conclude that it is not true, its unreality being granted? That would be a mistake. We live in times when everything can happen—we might almost say everything has happened. If our story does not seem to be true to-day, it may seem so to-morrow, thanks to the resources of science, which are the wealth of the future. No one would think of classing it as legendary. Besides, one does not invent legends at the close of this practical and positive nineteenth century; neither in Brittany, the country of the ferocious Korrigans; nor in Scotland, the land of the brownies and gnomes; nor in Norway, the land of ases, elfs, sylphs, and valkyries; nor even in Transylvania, where the Carpathian scenery lends itself so naturally to every psychagogic evocation. But at the same time it is as well to note that Transylvania is still much attached to the superstitions of the early ages.

These provinces of furthest Europe, M. de Gérando has described them, M. Elisée Reclus has visited them. Neither have said anything of the strange story on which this romance is founded. Did they know of it? Perhaps; but they did not wish to add to the belief in it. We are sorry for it; for if they had related it, one would have done so with the precision of an annalist, and the other with that instinctive poetry with which all his tales of travels are imbued. But as neither of them has told it, I will try to do so for them.

On the 29th of May a shepherd was watching his flock on the edge of a green plateau at the foot of Retyezat, which dominates a fertile valley, thickly wooded with straight-stemmed trees, and enriched with cultivation. This elevated plateau, open, unsheltered, the north-west winds sweep during the winter as closely as the barber's razor. It is said in the country that they shave it—and they do so, almost.

This shepherd had nothing arcadian in his costume, nor bucolic in his attitude. He was neither Daphnis, nor Arnyntas, nor Tityrus, nor Lycidas, nor Melibœus. The Lignon did not murmur at his feet, which were encased in thick wooden shoes; it was only the Wallachian Syl whose clear, pastoral waters were worthy of flowing through the meanderings of the romance of Astrea.

Frik, Frik of the village of Werst—such was the name of this rustic shepherd—was as roughly clothed as his sheep, but quite well enough for the hole, at the entrance of the village, where sheep and pigs lived in a state of revolting filth.

The *immanum pecus* fed then under the care of the said Frik—*immanior ipse*. Stretched on a hillock carpeted with grass, he slept with one eye open, his big pipe in his mouth; and now and then he gave a shrill whistle to his dogs when some sheep strayed away from the pasturage, or else he gave a more powerful blast which awoke the multiple echoes of the mountain.

It was four o'clock in the afternoon. The sun was sinking towards the horizon. A few summits whose bases were bathed in floating mist were standing out clear in the east. Towards the south-west two breaks in the chain allowed a slanting column of rays to enter the ring like a luminous jet passing through a half open door.

This orographic system belongs to the wildest part of Transylvania, known as the county of Klausenburg, or Kolosvar.

A curious fragment of the Austrian Empire is this Transylvania, "Erdely," in Magyar, which means the country of forests. It is bounded by Hungary on the north, Wallachia on the south, Moldavia on the west. Extending over sixty thousand square kilometres, about six millions of hectares, nearly the ninth of France, it is a kind of Switzerland, but half as large again, and no more populous. With its table-lands under cultivation, its luxuriant pasturages, its capriciously carved valleys, its frowning summits, Transylvania, streaked by the plutonic ramifications of the Carpathians, is furrowed by numerous watercourses flowing to swell the Theiss and the superb Danube, the Iron Gates of which, a few miles to the south, close the defile of the Balkan chain on the frontier of Hungary and the Ottoman Empire.

Such is this ancient country of Dacia, conquered by Trajan in the first century of the Christian Era. The independence it enjoyed under Jean Zapoly and his successors up to 1699, ended with Leopold the First, who annexed it to Austria. But such was its political constitution that it remained the common abode of the races which elbow each other but never mingle—Wallachians, or Roumans, Hungarians, Tsiganes, Szeklers of Moldavian origin, and also Saxons, whom time and circumstances will end by Magyarizing to the advantage of Transylvanian unity.

To which of these types did the shepherd Frik belong?

Was he a degenerate descendant of the ancient Dacians? He would not have found it easy to say so, to judge by his tumbled hair, his begrimed face, his bristly beard, his thick eyebrows, like two red-haired brushes, his bluish eyes, bluish or greenish, the humid corners of which were marked with the wrinkles of old age. He must have been sixty-five—you would never have guessed him less. But he was big, hardy, upright under his yellowish cloak, which was not as shaggy as his chest; and a painter would not have lost the chance of sketching him, when he was wearing his grass hat, a true wisp of straw, and resting on his crook as motionless as a rock.

Just as the rays penetrated through the break in the west, Frik turned over. His half-closed hand he made into a telescope, as he had already made it into a speaking-trumpet, to make his voice heard at a distance, and he looked through it attentively.

In the clear of the horizon, a good mile away, lay a group of buildings, with their outlines much softened by the distance. This old castle occupied on an isolated shoulder of the Vulkan range the upper part of a table-land called the Orgall Plateau. In the bright light the castle stood out with the clearness displayed in stereoscopic views. But, nevertheless, the shepherd's eye must have been endowed with great power of vision to be able to make out any detail in that distant mass.

Suddenly he exclaimed, as he shook his head,—

"Old castle! Old castle! You may well stand firm on your foundation. Three years more and you will have ceased to exist, for your beech-tree has only three branches left."

This beech-tree, planted at the extremity of one of the bastions of the enclosure, stood out black against the sky, and would have been almost invisible at that distance to any one else than Frik. The explanation of the shepherd's words, which were caused by a legend relative to the castle, we will give in due time.

"Yes," he repeated, "three branches. There were four yesterday, but the fourth has fallen during the night. I can only count three at the fork. No more than three, old castle—no more than three!"

If we attack a shepherd on his ideal side, the imagination readily takes him for a dreamy, contemplative being: he converses with the planets, he confers with the stars, he reads in the skies. In reality he is generally a stupid, ignorant brute. But public credulity easily credits him with supernatural gifts: he practises sorcery; according to his humour he can call up good fortune or bad, and scatter it among man and beast—or, what comes to the same thing, he sells sympathetic powder, and you can buy from him philtres and formulas. Can he not make the furrows barren by throwing into them enchanted stones? Can he not make sheep sterile by merely casting on them the evil eye? These superstitions are of all times and all countries. Even in the most civilized lands, one will never meet a shepherd without giving him some friendly word, some significant greeting, saluting him by the name of "pastor" to which he clings. A touch of the hat affords an escape from malign influences, and on the roads of Transylvania it is no more omitted than elsewhere.

Frik, then, was regarded as a sorcerer, a caller-up of apparitions. According to him the vampires and stryges obeyed him; if you were to believe him, these were to be met with at the setting of the moon, as on dark nights in other countries you see the great bissext astride on the arms of the mill talking with the wolves or dreaming in the starlight.

Frik profited by all this. He sold charms and counter charms. But, be it noted, he was as credulous as his believers; and if he did not believe in his own witchcraft, he believed in the legends of his country.

There is nothing surprising therefore in his prophecy regarding the approaching disappearance of the old castle, now that the beech was reduced to three branches, or in his at once setting out to bear the news to Werst.

After mustering his flock by bellowing loudly through a long trumpet of white wood, he took the road to the village. His dogs followed him, hurrying on the sheep as they did so—two mongrel demi-griffins, snarling and ferocious,

3

who seemed fitter to eat the sheep than to guard them. He had a hundred rams and ewes, a dozen yearlings, the rest three and four years old.

The flock belonged to the judge of Werst, the biro Koltz, who paid the commune a large sum for pasturage, and who thought a good deal of his shepherd Frik, knowing him to be a skilful shearer and well acquainted with the treatment of such maladies as thrush, giddiness, fluke, rot, foot rot, and other cattle ailments.

The flock moved in a compact mass, the bell-wether at the head, making the bell heard above the bleating.

As he left the pasture Frik took a wide footpath bordered by spacious fields, in which waved magnificent ears of corn, very long in the straw and high on the stalk; and several plantations, of koukouroutz, which is the maize of the country. The road led to the edge of a forest of firs and spruces, fresh and gloomy beneath their branches. Lower down the Syl flowed along its luminous course, filtering through the pebbles in its bed, and bearing the logs of wood from the sawmills upstream.

Dogs and sheep stopped on the right bank of the river and began to drink greedily, pushing the reeds aside to do so.

Werst was not more than three gunshots away, beyond a thick plantation of willows formed of well-grown trees, and not of stunted pollards which only grow bushy for a few feet above their roots. These willows stretched a way up to Vulkan Hill, of which the village of the same name occupied a projection on the southern slope of the Plesa range.

The fields were now deserted. It is only at nightfall that the labourers return home, and Frik as he went along had no traditional "good night" to exchange. When his flock had satisfied their thirst, he was about to enter the fold of the valley when a man appeared at the bend of the Syl, some fifty yards downstream.

"Hallo, friend!" said he to the shepherd.

He was one of those pedlars who travel from market to market in the district. They are to be met with in the towns and all the villages. In making themselves understood they have no difficulty, for they speak all languages. Was this one an Italian, a Saxon, or a Wallachian? No one could say, but he was unmistakably a Jew—tall, thin, hook-nosed, with a pointed beard, a prominent forehead, and keen, glittering eyes.

This pedlar dealt in telescopes, thermometers, barometers, and small clocks. What he did not carry in the bag strongly strapped over his shoulder, he bung from his neck and his belt, so that he was quite a travelling stall.

Probably this Jew had the usual respect for shepherds and the salutary fear they inspire. He shook Frik by the hand. Then in the Rouman language, which is a mixture of Latin and Sclave, he said with a foreign accent,—

"Are you getting on, all right, friend?"

"Yes—considering the weather," replied Frik.

"Then you must be doing well to-day, for the weather is beautiful."

"And I shall not be doing well to-morrow, for it will rain."

"It will rain?" said the pedlar. "Then it rains without clouds in your country?"

"The clouds will come to-night—and from yonder, the bad side of the mountain."

"How do you know that?"

"By the wool of my sheep, which is harsh and dry as tanned leather."

"Then it will be all the worse for those who are on a long journey."

"And all the better for those who stay near home."

"Then you have a home, shepherd?"

"Have you any children?" said Frik.

"No."

"Are you married?"

"No."

And Frik asked this because in this country it is the custom to do so of those you meet. He continued,—

"Where do you come from, pedlar?"

"From Hermanstadt."

Hermanstadt is one of the principal villages of Transylvania. On leaving it you find the valley of the Hungarian Syl, which flows down to the town of Petroseny.

"And you are going?"

"To Kolosvar."

To reach Kolosvar you have to ascend the valley of the Maros, and then by Karlsburg along the lower slopes of the Bihar mountains you reach the capital of the country. It is a walk of twenty miles only.

These vendors of thermometers, barometers, and cheap jewellery always seem to be a peculiar people and somewhat Hoffmanesque in their bearing. It is part of their trade. They sell time and weather in all forms—the time which flies, the weather which is, and the weather which will be—just as other packmen sell baskets and drapery. They are commercial travellers for the house of Saturn & Co., of the sign of the Golden Shoe. And doubtless this was the effect the Jew produced on Frik, who gazed not without astonishment at this display of things which were new to him, the use of which he did not know.

"I say, pedlar," said he, stretching out his arm, "what is the use of all this trumpery which rattles at your belt like a lot of old bones?"

"These things are valuable," said the pedlar; "they are of use to everybody."

"To everybody?" said Frik, winking his eye, "even to shepherds?"

"Even to shepherds."

"What is the use of this machine?"

"This machine," answered the Jew, putting a thermometer into his hands, "will tell you if it is hot or cold."

"Ah, friend! I can tell that when I am sweating under my tunic, or shivering under my overcoat."

Evidently that was enough for a shepherd who did not trouble himself about the wherefore of science.

"And this big watch with a needle?" continued he, pointing to an aneroid.

"That is not a watch, but an instrument which will tell you if it will be fine to-morrow or if it will rain."

"Really?"

"Really."

"Good," said Frik, "I don't want that even if it only costs a kreutzer. I have only to look at the clouds trailing along the mountains or racing over the higher peaks, and I can tell you what the weather will be a day in advance. Look, do you see that mist which seems to rise from the ground? Well, I tell you it means water for to-morrow!"

And in fact the shepherd, who was a great observer of the weather, could do very well without a barometer.

"I will not ask you if you want a clock," continued the pedlar.

"A clock! I have one which goes by itself and hangs over my head. That is the sun up there. Look you, friend, when it is over the peak of Roduk it is noon; when it looks at me across the gap of Egelt it is six o'clock. My sheep know it as well as I do, and my dogs know it as well as my sheep. You can keep your clocks."

"Then," said the pedlar, "if my only customers were shepherds, I should have hard work to make a fortune. And so you want nothing?"

"Nothing at all."

Besides which all these low-priced goods were of very poor workmanship: the barometers never agreed as to its being changeable weather or fair, the clock-hands made the hours too long or the minutes too short—in fact they were pure rubbish. The shepherd suspected this, perhaps, and did not care to become a buyer. But just as he was taking up his stick again, he caught sight of a sort of tube hanging from the pedlar's strap.

"What do you do with that tube?"

"That tube is not a tube."

"Is it a blunderbuss?"

"No," said the Jew, "it is a telescope."

It was one of those common telescopes which magnify the objects five or six times, or bring them as near, which produces the same result.

Frik unhooked the instrument, he looked at it, he handled it, and opened and shut it.

Then he shook his head

"A telescope?" he asked.

"Yes, shepherd, and a good one, and one that will make you see a long way off."

"Oh! I have good eyes, my friend. When the air is clear I can see the rocks on the top of Retyezat and the farthest trees in the Vulkan valleys."

"Without winking?"

"Without winking. It is the dew which makes me do that, and my sleeping from night to morning under the star-lit sky. That is the sort of thing to keep your pupils clean."

"What—the dew?" said the pedlar. "It might perhaps make the blind—"

"Not the shepherds."

"Quite so! But if you have good eyes, mine are better when I get them at the end of that telescope."

"That remains to be seen."

"Put yours to it now!"

"Mine?"

"Try."

"Will that cost me anything?" asked Frik suspiciously.

"Nothing at all, unless you buy the machine."

Being reassured on this point, Frik took the telescope, the tubes of which were adjusted by the pedlar. Shutting his left eye as directed, he applied his right eye to the eye piece.

At first he looked towards Vulkan Hill and then up towards Plesa. That done, he lowered the instrument and brought it to bear on the village of Werst.

"Ah! ah!" he said. "Perhaps you are right. It does carry farther than my eyes. There is the main road, I recognize the people. There is Nic Deck, the forester, coming home with his haversack on his back and his gun over his shoulder."

"I told you so," said the pedlar.

"Yes, yes, that is really Nic!" said the shepherd. "And who is the girl who is coming out of Koltz's house, with the red petticoat and the black bodice, as if to get in front of him?"

"Keep on looking, shepherd. You will soon recognize the girl, as you did the young man."

"Ah! yes! It is Miriota—the lovely Miriota! Ah! the lovers, the lovers! This time I have got them at the end of my tube, and I shall not lose one of their little goings on!"

"What do you say to the telescope?"

"Eh? It does make you see far!"

As Frik was looking through a telescope for the first time, it follows that Werst was one of the most backward villages of the country of Klausenburg; and that this was so we shall soon see.

"Come, shepherd," continued the pedlar, "look again; look farther than Werst. The village is too near us. Look beyond, farther beyond, I tell you!"

"Shall I have to pay any more?"

"No more."

"Good! I will look towards the Hungarian Syl! Yes. There is the clock-tower at Livadzel. I recognize it by the cross which has lost one arm. And, beyond, in the valley, among the pines, I see the spire of Petroseny with its weathercock of zinc with the open beak as if it were calling its chickens; and, beyond, there is that tower pointing up amid the trees. But I suppose, pedlar, it is all at the same price?"

"All the same price, shepherd."

Frik turned the telescope towards the plateau of Orgall; then with it he followed the curtain of forests darkening the slopes of Plesa, and the field of the objective framed the distant outline of the village.

"Yes!" he exclaimed, "the fourth branch is on the ground. I had seen aright. And no one will get it to make a torch of it for the night of St. John. Nobody, not even me! It would be to risk both body and soul. But do not trouble yourself about it. There is one who knows how to gather it to-night for his infernal fire— and that is the Chort!"

The Chort being the devil when he is invoked in the language of the country.

Perhaps the Jew might have demanded an explanation of these incomprehensible words, as he was not a native of the village of Werst or its environs, had not Frik exclaimed in a voice of terror mingled with surprise,—

"What is that mist escaping from the donjon? Is it a mist? No! One would say it was a smoke! It is not possible. For hundreds and hundreds of years no smoke has come from the chimneys of the castle!"

"If you see a smoke over there, shepherd, there is a smoke."

"No, pedlar, no. It is the glass of your machine which is misty."

"Clean it."

"And when I have cleaned it—"

Frik shifted the telescope, and, having rubbed the glasses, he replaced it at his eye.

It was undoubtedly a smoke streaming from the upper part of the donjon. It mounted high in the air and mingled with the higher vapours.

Frik remained motionless and silent. All his attention was concentrated on the castle, from which the rising shadow began to touch the level of the plateau of Orgall.

Suddenly he lowered the telescope, and, thrusting his band into the pouch he wore under his frock, he said,—

"How much do you want for your tube?"

"A florin and a half!" said the pedlar.

And he would have sold the telescope for a florin if Frik had shown any desire to bargain for it. But the shepherd said not a word. Evidently under the influence of an astonishment as sudden as it was inexplicable, he plunged his hand to the bottom of his wallet and drew out the money.

"Are you buying the telescope for yourself?" asked the pedlar.

"No; for my master."

"And he will pay you back?"

"Yes the two florins it costs me."

"What! The two florins?"

"Eh! Certainly! That and no less. Good evening, my friend!"

"Good evening, shepherd."

And Frik, whistling his dogs and urging on his flock, struck off rapidly in the direction of Werst.

The Jew, looking at him as he went, shook his head, as if he had been doing a trade with a madman.

"If I had known that," he murmured, "I should have charged him more for that telescope."

Then he adjusted his burden on his belt and shoulders and resumed his journey to Karlsburg along the right bank of the Syl.

Where did he go? It matters little. He passed out of this story. We shall meet with him no more.

CHAPTER II.

It matters not whether we are dealing with native rocks piled up by natural means in distant geological epochs, or with constructions due to the hand of man over which the breath of time has passed, the effect is much the same when viewed from a few miles off. Unworked stone and worked stone may easily be confounded. From afar, the same colour, the same lineaments, the same deviations of line in the perspective, the same uniformity of tint under the grey patina of centuries.

And so it was with this castle, otherwise known as the Castle of the Carpathians. To distinguish the indefinite outlines of this structure on the plateau of Orgall, which crowns the left of Vulkan Hill, was impossible. It did not stand out in relief from the background of mountains. What might have been taken as a donjon was only a stony mound; what might be supposed to be a curtain with its battlements might be only a rocky crest. The mass was vague, floating, uncertain. And in the opinion of many tourists the Castle of the Carpathians existed only in the imagination of the country people.

Evidently the simplest means of assuring yourself as to its existence would have been to have bargained with a guide from Vulkan or Werst, to have gone up the valley, scaled the ridge, and visited the buildings. But a guide would have been as difficult to find as the road leading to the castle. In the valley of both

Syls no one would have agreed to be guide to a traveller, for no matter what remuneration, to the Castle of the Carpathians.

What they would have seen of this ancient habitation in the field of a telescope more powerful and better focussed than the trumpery thing bought by the shepherd Frik on account of his master Koltz, was this:—

Some 800 or 900 feet in the rear of Vulkan Hill lay a grey enclosure, covered with a mass of wall plants, and extending for from 400 to 500 feet along the irregularities of the plateau; at each end were two angular bastions, in the right of which grew the famous beech close by a slender watch-tower or look-out with a pointed roof; on the left a few patches of wall, strengthened by flying buttresses, supporting the tower of a chapel, the cracked bell of which was often sounded in high winds to the great alarm of the district; in the midst, crowned by its crenellated platform, a heavy, formidable donjon, with three rows of leaded windows, the first storey of which was surrounded by a circular terrace; on the platform a long metal spire, ornamented with a feudal virolet, or weathercock, stationary with rust, which a last puff of the north-west wind had set pointing to the south-east.

As to what was contained in this enclosure, if there was any habitable building within, if a drawbridge or a postern gave admittance to it, had been unknown for a number of years. In fact, although the Castle of the Carpathians was in better preservation than it seemed to be, an infectious terror, doubled by superstition, protected it as much as it had formerly been by its basilisks, its grasshoppers, its bombards, its culverins, its thunderers, and other engines of mediæval artillery.

But, nevertheless, the Castle of the Carpathians was well worth visiting by tourists and antiquaries. Its situation on the crest of the Orgall plateau was exceptionally fine. From the upper platform of the keep, or donjon, the view extended to the farthest point of the mountains. In the rear undulated the lofty chain, so capriciously spurred, which serves as the frontier of Wallachia. In front lay the sinuous defile of the Vulkan, the only practicable route between the frontier provinces. Beyond the valley of the two Syls lay the towns of Livadzel, Lonyai, Petroseny, and Petrilla, grouped at the mouths of the shafts by which this rich coal-basin is worked. In the distance lay an admirable series of ridges, wooded to their bases, green on their flanks, barren on their summits, commanded by the rugged peaks of Retyezat and Paring. Far away beyond the valley of the Hatszeg and the course of the Maros, appeared the distant mist-clad outlines of the Alps of Central Transylvania.

Hereabouts the depression of the ground formerly formed a lake into which the two Syls flowed before they found a passage through the chain. Nowadays this depression is a coal-field with its advantages and inconveniences: the tall brick chimneys rise amid the poplars, pines, and beeches, and black fumes poison the air which once was saturated with the perfumes of fruit-trees and flowers. But at the time of our story, although industry was holding the mining district under its iron hand, nothing had been lost of the country's wild character which was its by nature.

The Castle of the Carpathians dated from the twelfth or thirteenth century. In those days, under the rule of the chiefs or voivodes, monasteries, churches, palaces, castles were fortified with as much care as the towns and villages. Lords and peasants had to secure themselves against aggression of all kinds. This state of affairs explains why the old fortifications of the castle, its bastions and its keep, gave it the appearance of a feudal building. What architect would have built on this plateau at this height? We know not, and the bold builder is unknown, unless it was the Rouman Manoli, so gloriously sung of in Wallachian legend, and who built at Curté d'Argis the celebrated castle of Rodolphe the Black.

Whatever doubts there might be as to the architect, there were none as to the family who owned the castle. The barons of Gortz had been lords of the country from time immemorial. They were mixed up in all the wars which ensanguined the Transylvanian fields; they fought against the Hungarians, the Saxons, the Szeklers; their name figures in the "cantices" and "doines," in which is perpetuated the memory of these disastrous times. For their motto they had the famous Wallachian proverb, *Da pe maorte*, "Give unto death;" and they gave; they poured out their blood for the cause of independence, the blood which came to them from the Romans their ancestors.

As we know, all their efforts of devotedness and sacrifice ended only in reducing the descendants of this valiant race to the most unworthy oppression. It no longer exists politically. Three heels have crushed it. But these Wallachians of Transylvania have not despaired of shaking off the yoke. The future belongs to them, and it is with unshakable confidence that they repeat these words in which are concentrated all their aspirations: "Roman no péré!" (the Rouman does not know how to perish).

Towards the middle of the nineteenth century the last representative of the lords of Gortz was Baron Rodolphe. Born at the Castle of the Carpathians, he had seen the family die away around him in the early years of his youth. When he was twenty-two years old he found himself alone in the world. His people had fallen off year by year, like the branches of the old beech-tree with which popular superstition associated the very existence of the castle. Without relatives, we might even say without friends, what could Baron Rodolphe do to occupy the leisure of this monotonous solitude that death had made around him? What were his tastes, his instincts, his aptitudes? It would not have been easy to discover any beyond an irresistible passion for music, particularly for the singing of the great artistes of the period. And so, after having entrusted the castle, then much dilapidated, to the care of a few old servants, he one day disappeared.

And, as was discovered later on, he had devoted his wealth, which was considerable, to visiting the chief lyrical centres of Europe, the theatres of Germany, France, and Italy, where he could indulge himself in his insatiable dilettante fancies. Was he an oddity, or a madman? The strangeness of his life led people to suppose so.

But the remembrance of his country was deeply engraven on the heart of the young lord of Gortz. In his distant wanderings he had not forgotten his Transylvanian birthplace. And he had returned to take part in one of the sanguinary revolts of the Roumanian peasantry against Hungarian oppression.

The descendants of the ancient Dacians were conquered, and their territory shared among the conquerors.

It was in consequence of this defeat that Baron Rodolphe finally left the Castle of the Carpathians, certain parts of which had already fallen into ruin. Death soon deprived the castle of its last servants and it was totally deserted. As to the Baron de Gortz, the report went that he had patriotically associated himself with the famous Rosza Sandor, an old highwayman, whom the war of independence had made a dramatic hero. Happily for him, at the close of the struggle Rodolphe de Gortz had separated from the band of the "betyar," and he had done wisely, for the old brigand had again become a robber, and ended by falling into the hands of the police, who shut him up in the prison of Szamos-Uyvar.

Nevertheless, another version was generally believed in in the country, to the effect that Baron Rodolphe had been killed during an encounter between Rosza Sandor and the custom-house officers on the frontier. This was not so, although the Baron de Gortz had never appeared at the castle since that time, and his death was generally taken for granted. But it is wise not to accept without considerable reserve the gossip of this credulous people.

A castle deserted, haunted, and mysterious. A vivid and ardent imagination had soon peopled it with phantoms; ghosts appeared in it, and spirits returned to it at all hours of the night. Such opinions are still common in certain superstitious countries of Europe, and Transylvania is one of the most superstitious.

Besides, how could the village of Werst put off its belief in the supernatural? The pope and the school master, the one charged with the education of the faithful, the other charged with the education of the children, taught their fables as openly as if they believed in them thoroughly. They affirmed, and even produced "corroborative evidence" that were-wolves prowled about the country; that vampires known as stryges, because they shrieked like stryges, quenched their thirst on human blood; that "staffii" lurked about ruins and became vindictive if something to eat and drink were not left for them every night. There were fairies, "babes" who should not be met with on Thursdays or Fridays, the two worst days in the week. In the depths of the forests, those enchanted forests, there wandered the "balauri," those gigantic dragons whose jaws gape up to the clouds, the "zmei" with vast wings, who carry away the daughters of the royal blood, and even those of meaner lineage when they are pretty! Here, it would seem, were a number of formidable monsters, and what is the good genius opposed to them in the popular imagination? Simply the "serpi de casa," the snake of the fireside, which lives at the back of the hearth, and whose healthy influence the peasant purchases by feeding him with the best milk.

If ever a castle was a fitting refuge for the creatures of this Roumanian mythology, was it not the Castle of the Carpathians? On that isolated plateau, inaccessible except from the left of Vulkan Hill, there could be no doubt that there lived dragons and fairies and stryges, and probably a few ghosts of the family of the barons of Gortz. And so it had an evil reputation, which it deserved, as they said. No one dared to visit it. It spread around it a terrible epidemic as an unhealthy marsh gives forth its pestilential emanations. Nothing could approach it within a quarter of a mile without risking its life in this world and its salvation in the next. At least so it was taught in the school of Magister Hermod.

But at the same time this state of things was to end eventually, and that as soon as no stone remained of the ancient stronghold of the barons of Gortz. And here it was that the legend came in.

If we were to believe the authorities of the village of Werst, the existence of the castle was bound up with that of the old beech-tree which grew in the bastion to the right of the enclosure. Since the departure of Rodolphe de Gortz, the people of the village, and more especially the shepherd Frik, had observed it— this beech-tree had lost one of its main branches every year. There were eighteen from the first fork when Baron Rodolphe was seen for the last time on the platform of the keep, and now the tree had only three. Consequently every branch that fell meant a year less in the castle's life. The fall of the last would mean the final dissolution; and then on the plateau of Orgall the remains of the Castle of the Carpathians would be sought in vain.

Evidently this was but one of those legends which spring up so readily in Roumanian imagination. In the first place it remained to be proved that this beech-tree did really lose one of its branches a year, although Frik did not hesitate to assert that it did, he who never lost sight of it while his flock pastured in the meadows of the Syl. Nevertheless, from the highest to the lowest of the people of Werst, none doubted that the castle had but three years to live, for only three branches could now be counted on the tutelary tree.

Thus it was that the shepherd had started on his return, to the village with the important news when there occurred the incident of the telescope.

Important news, very important news in fact! Smoke had appeared above the donjon! That which his eyes alone had not been able to notice, Frik Lad distinctly seen with the pedlar's telescope. It was no vapour but real smoke which had risen into the clouds! And yet the castle was deserted. For a long time no one had entered the gate, which was doubtless shut, nor crossed the drawbridge, which was doubtless up. If it were inhabited it could only be by supernatural beings. But what use could spirits have for a fire in the rooms of the keep? Was it a fire in a room? Was it a kitchen fire? Really it was inexplicable.

Frik hurried his sheep along the road; at his voice the dogs urged the flock up the rising track, the dust of which had been laid by the evening moisture.

A few peasants, delayed in the fields, greeted him as he passed, and he scarcely replied to them. And consequently there was much uneasiness, for if you would avoid evil influences it is not enough to say "Good evening" to a shepherd, but the shepherd must say it to you. And Frik did not appear much inclined to do so, as he hurried on with his haggard eyes, his curious gait, and his excited gestures. The wolves and the bears might have walked off with half his flock without his noticing it.

The first who learnt the news was Judge Koltz. From afar Frik saw him and shouted,

"There is a fire at the castle, master!"

"What do you say?"

"I say what there is."

"Have you gone mad?"

And how could a fire break out in such a heap of old stones? As well assert that Negoi, the highest peak of the Carpathians, had been devoured by flames. It would have been no more absurd.

"You suppose that the castle is on fire?" asked Master Koltz.

"If it is not on fire, it smokes."

"It is some vapour."

"No; it is smoke. Come and see!"

And they went into the middle of the main road of the village; near the terrace, from which the castle could be observed.

When they got there Frik held out the telescope to Master Koltz.

Evidently the use of this instrument was no more known to him than it had been to his shepherd.

"What is that?" he said.

"A machine I bought for you for two florins, master, and it is well worth four."

"Of whom?"

"A pedlar."

"And what is it to do?"

"Put it to your eye, look straight at the castle, and you will see."

The judge levelled the telescope at the castle and looked through it for some time.

Yes! There was certainly smoke rising from one of the chimneys of the donjon. At this moment it was being blown away by the breeze and floating up the flank of the mountain.

"Smoke!" said Master Koltz, astonished. But now he and Frik had been joined by Miriota and the forester, Nic Deck, who had been indoors for some time.

"What is the use of this?" asked the young man, taking the telescope.

"To see with afar off," said the shepherd.

"Are you joking?"

"Joking? Hardly an hour ago I saw you coming down the road into Werst. You and—"

He did not finish his sentence. Miriota had blushed and lowered her pretty eyes. After all, there was no harm in an honest young girl going to meet her betrothed.

Both of them took the famous telescope, and looked through it at the castle.

Meanwhile half a dozen neighbours had arrived on the terrace, and, after many questions as to what it all meant, took a look through the telescope in turn.

"A smoke! A smoke at the castle!" said one.

"Perhaps the lightning has struck the donjon!" said another.

"Has there been any thunder?" asked Master Koltz, addressing Frik.

"Not a sound for a week," said the shepherd.

And the good folks could not have been more startled if a crater had opened on the summit of Retyezat to give passage to the subterranean vapours.

CHAPTER III.

The village of Werst is of so little importance that most maps do not indicate its position. In administrative rank it is even below its neighbour called Vulkan, from the name of that portion of the Plesa range on which both are picturesquely situated.

At the present time, when the opening up of the coal field has increased the importance of the towns of Petroseny, Livadzel, and others, a few miles off, neither Vulkan nor Werst has received the least advantage from their proximity to a great industrial centre. What the villages were fifty years ago—what they will doubtless be half a century hence—they are still; and, according to Elisée Reclus, a good half of the Vulkan population consists of "people engaged in watching the frontier—custom house officers, gendarmes, revenue officers, and quarantine attendants." Omit the gendarmes and the revenue officers, add a larger proportion of agriculturists, and you will have the population of Werst, consisting of a few hundred inhabitants.

It is a street, this village, nothing but a wide street, the uphill nature of which makes the ascent and descent laborious enough along the road. It serves as the natural thoroughfare between the Wallachian and Transylvanian frontier. Through it pass the cattle and sheep and pigs, the dealers in fresh provisions, fruits, and cereals, the few travellers who venture through the defile instead of taking the Kolosvar and Maros valley railways.

Nature has assuredly generously endowed the district between the mountains of Bihar, Retyezat, and Paring. Rich in the fertility of its soil, it is also rich in its underground wealth. There are salt-mines at Thorda with an annual output of more than twenty thousand tons: Mount Parajd, measuring seven kilometres in circumference at its dome, is entirely formed of chloride of sodium; the mines of Torotzko yield lead, galena, mercury, and especially iron, the beds of which were worked in the tenth century; at Vayda Hunyad are mines whose products can be turned into steel of superior quality; there are coal mines easily worked in the upper strata of the lacustrine valleys of the districts of Hatszeg, Livadzel, and Petroseny, a vast deposit, estimated to contain two hundred and fifty million tons; and, finally, there are gold-mines at Offenbanya, at Topanfalva, the region of the gold-seekers, where thousands of primitive mills are working the sands of Verès-Patak, "The Transylvanian Pactolus," and exporting every year about two million francs' worth of the precious metal.

Here is a district that would seem to be greatly favoured by nature, and yet its wealth is of very little profit to its population. If the more important centres, like Torotzko, Petroseny, and Lonyai, possess a few establishments suited to the comfortable conditions of modern industrial life; if they have regular buildings laid out with rule and line, and outhouses and shops, real workmen's towns in fact; if they have a certain number of houses with balconies and verandahs, that is not the case at Vulkan or at Werst.

Some sixty houses, irregularly clustering along the only street, capped with a fanciful roof, the ridge overhanging the mud wall, the front towards the garden, an attic with a skylight as a top storey, a dilapidated barn as an annexe: a stable all awry, covered with straw; here and there a well surmounted by a beam from which hangs a bucket; two or three ponds which run over during a storm; streams, of which the tortuous ruts indicate the course; such is the village of Werst, built on both sides of the road between the slanting slopes of the hill. But it is all very fresh and attractive; there are flowers at the doors and windows; curtains of verdure screening the walls; plants in disorder mingling with the old gold of the thatch; poplars, elms, beeches, pines, maples, climbing above the houses as high as they can. Beyond are the zigzagged flanks of the hills, and in the background the tops of the mountains, blue in the distance, and mingling their blue with the sky.

Neither German nor Hungarian is spoken at Werst, nor in any of this part of Transylvania; the people speak Roumanian—even the gipsies do so, of whom a few families are established rather than camped in the different villages of the country. These strangers adopt the language of the country as they adopt the religion. Those of Werst form a sort of little clan, under the authority of a voivode, with their huts, their "barakas" with pointed roofs, their legions of children, so different in the manners and regularity of their life from those of their congeners who wander about Europe. They even belong to the Greek

Church, and conform to the religion of the Christians among whom they have settled. As religious head Werst has a pope, who resides at Vulkan, and superintends the two villages, which are only half a mile apart.

Civilization is like air or water. Wherever there is a passage, be it only a fissure, it will penetrate and modify the conditions of a country. But it must be admitted that no fissure has yet been found through this southern portion of the Carpathians. Vulkan, as Elisée Reclus says, is "the last post of civilization in the valley of the Wallachian Syl, and we need not be astonished at Werst being one of the most backward villages of the county of Kolosvar. And how could it be otherwise in these places, where everyone is born and lives and dies without ever leaving them?

But perhaps you will say there is a schoolmaster and a judge at Werst? Yes, without doubt. But Magister Hermod was only able to teach what he knew—that is, to read a little, to write a little, to reckon a little. His personal instruction did not go beyond that. Of science, history, geography, literature, he knew nothing beyond the popular songs and legends of the surrounding country. In that respect his memory was richly stored. He was strong in matters of romance, and the few scholars of the village gained great profit from his lessons.

As to the judge, we may as well say something concerning this chief magistrate of Werst.

The biro, Master Koltz, was a little man, of from fifty-five to sixty years old, a Roumanian by birth, his hair close cut and grey, his moustache still black, his eyes more gentle than fiery. Solidly built, like a mountaineer, he wore the large felt hat on his head, the high belt with ornamental buckle round his waist, the sleeveless vest, and the short baggy breeches tucked into his high leather boots. As much mayor as judge, for his functions obliged him to intervene in the many disputes between neighbour and neighbour, he was chiefly occupied in administering his village with a great show of authority, and not without some benefit to his purse. In fact, all transactions, purchases or sales, were subject to a tax for his benefit, to say nothing of the tolls with which travellers for pleasure or trade filled his pocket.

This lucrative position kept Master Koltz in easy circumstances. If most of the peasants of the country were ground down by the usury of the Israelitish money-lenders, who were the real proprietors of the soil, the biro had managed to escape. His goods were free from hypothecations, "intabulations," as they are called in the country; and he owed nothing. He would rather have lent than borrowed, and would certainly have done so with-out fleecing the poor people. He owned several pasturages, good grazing grounds for his flocks; lands under fair cultivation, although he would have nothing to do with the new methods; vineyards which flattered his vanity when he walked down the lines of stocks covered with the grapes he sold at a goodly profit, although he retained a fair proportion for his private consumption.

It need not be said that the house of Master Koltz was the best in the village, at the angle of the terrace which crossed the long road as it ascended. A stone house, if you please, with its façade continued round on to the garden; its door between the third and fourth windows, with the festoons of verdure bordering the gutter with their slender branchlets; with the two great beech-trees spreading their boughs above the flowery thatch. Behind lay a fine orchard, with its beds of vegetables like a chess board, and its rows of fruit-trees skirting the slope of the hill. Inside the house were fine clean rooms, some to dine in, some to sleep in, with their painted furniture, tables, beds, benches and stools, their sideboards, on which shone the pots and dishes; the beams of the ceiling, from which hung vases decorated with ribbons and gaily-coloured stuffs; the heavy coffers, covered with cloths and quilts, which served as chests and cupboards, the white walls, the highly-coloured portraits of Roumanian patriots—amongst others the popular hero of the fifteenth century, the voivode Vayda-Hunyad.

It was a charming house, which would have been too large for a man by himself. But Master Koltz was not alone. A widower for twelve years, he had a daughter, the lovely Miriota, who was much admired from Werst to Vulkan, and even beyond. She might have been called by one of those strange Pagan names, Florica, Darna, Danritia, which are much in honour in Wallachian families. But no! she was Miriota; that is to say, the little sheep. But she had grown, this little sheep, and was now a graceful girl of twenty, fair, with brown eyes, a gentle look, charming features, and a pleasing figure. In truth, she could not look other than attractive, with her chemisette embroidered with red thread up to the collar and on the wrists and on the shoulders, her petticoat clasped by a belt with silver buckles, her "catrinza," or double apron, with red and blue stripes, knotted to her waist, her little boots of yellow leather, the light handkerchief on her head, her long hair floating behind her, the plait of which was ornamented with a ribbon or a metal clasp.

Yes! a handsome girl was Miriota Koltz, and—no harm to her—she was rich, that is, for this village lost in the depths of the Carpathians. A good manager? Undoubtedly; for she managed her father's house in intelligent fashion. Was she educated? Yes; at Magister Hermod's school she had learnt to read, to write, to cipher, and she ciphered, wrote, and read correctly; but she had not been pushed very far—and there were reasons for it. On the other hand, she knew about as much as was to be known of the Transylvanian traditions and sagas. She knew as much as her master. She knew the legend of Leany-Ko, the Rock of the Virgin, in which a rather fanciful princess escapes from the pursuit of the Tartars; the legend of the Dragon's Cave in the Valley of the King's Stairs; the legend of the fortress of Deva, which was built in the "days of the Fairies;" the legend of the Detunata, the "Thunderclap," that famous basaltic mountain like a gigantic stone fiddle, on which the devil plays on stormy nights; the legend of Retyezat, with its summit cut down by a witch; the legend of the Valley of Thorda, which was cleft by the stroke of the sword of Saint Ladislas. We must confess that Miriota believed in all these mythological fictions; but she was none the less a charming and amiable girl.

A good many young men of the district found her so, even without considering that she was the only heiress of the biro, Master Koltz, the first magistrate of Werst. But there was no use in paying her attentions. Was she not already engaged to Nicolas Deck?

A handsome type of Roumanian was this Nicolas, or, rather, Nic Deck, twenty-five years of age, tall, strong in constitution, head well set on his shoulders, hair black, covered by the white kolpak, look clear and frank, bearing himself well under his vest of lambskin embroidered with needlework, well set on his slender legs, legs as of a deer, and an air of determination in his gait and gestures. He as a forester by trade; that is to say, almost as much a soldier as a civilian. As he owned a little land under cultivation in the environs of Werst he was approved of by the father, and as he was a good-looking, well-made fellow he was approved of by the daughter, with whom he was deeply in love. He would not allow anyone to attempt to rival him, nor to look at her too closely—and no one thought of doing so.

The marriage of Nic Deck and Miriota Koltz was to take place in a fortnight, towards the middle of the approaching month. On that occasion the village would hold a general holiday. Master Koltz would do the thing properly. He was no miser. If he liked getting money, he did not refuse to spend it when opportunity offered.

When the ceremony was over Nic Deck would take up his residence in the house which would be his when the biro was gone; and when Miriota knew he was near her, perhaps she would cease to fear, as she heard the creak of a door or the rattling of a window in the long winter nights, that some phantom escaped from her favourite legends was about to put in an appearance.

To complete the list of the notables of Werst, we must mention two more, and these not the least important, the schoolmaster and the doctor.

Magister Hermod was a big man in spectacles, about forty-five years old, having always between his lips the curved stem of his pipe with the porcelain bowl, his hair thin and disordered on a flattish head, his face hairless, with a twitching in the left cheek. His great occupation was cutting the pens of his pupils, whom he forbade to use steel pens on principle. But how he lengthened the nibs with his old pointed pocket-knife! With what precision and winking of his eyes did he give the final touch by cutting the point! Above everything good handwriting—to that all his efforts were directed; it was to that that a schoolmaster careful of his mission should urge his pupils. Instruction was of secondary importance—and we know what Magister Hermod taught and what the generations of boys and girls learnt on the benches of his school.

And now for the turn of Doctor Patak. What! a doctor at Werst, and yet the village still believed in the supernatural?

Yes; but we may as well be clear as to the title borne by Doctor Patak as we had to be regarding that borne by Judge Koltz.

Patak was a little man with a prominent corporation, short and fat, aged about forty-five, ostensibly acting as medical adviser in Werst and its neighbourhood. With his imperturbable self-confidence, his deafening loquacity, he inspired no less confidence than the shepherd Frik and that is not saying little. He dealt in consultations and drugs; but so harmless were they that they made no worse the petty ailments of his patients, who would have got well had they been left to themselves. People are healthy enough in these parts; the air is of the first quality, epidemic maladies are there unknown; if people die it is because they must, even in this privileged corner of Transylvania. As to Doctor Patak—yes, they called him doctor!—although he was accepted as such, he had had no education either in medicine or in pharmacy or in anything. He was merely an old quarantine attendant, whose occupation consisted in looking after the travellers detained on the frontier for health purposes. Nothing more. That, it appeared, was enough for the easy-going people of Werst.

It could be added—and there is nothing surprising in it—that Doctor Patak was a strong spirit, as is usually the case with one who has to look after other people. And he believed in none of the superstitions current in the Carpathian district, not even in those that were cherished in the village. He laughed at them, he made fun of them. And when he was told that no one had dared to approach the castle from time immemorial, he would say,—

"You must not dare me to visit the old hovel!"

But as they did not dare him, as they carefully kept from daring him, Doctor Patak had never been there, and with the help of credulity the Castle of the Carpathians remained enveloped in impenetrable mystery.

CHAPTER IV.

In a few minutes the news brought by the shepherd had spread in the village. Master Koltz, carrying the precious telescope, went back into his house, followed by Nic Deck and Miriota. There now remained on the terrace only Frik surrounded by about twenty men, women, and children, among whom were a few Tsiganes, who were not the least excited among the Werst population. They surrounded Frik, they bombarded him with questions, and the shepherd replied with the superb importance of a man who had just seen something quite extraordinary.

"Yes!" he repeated, "the castle was smoking, it still smokes, and it will smoke until not one stone of it remains on another."

"But who could have lighted the fire?" asked an old woman with her hands clasped.

"The Chort!" said Frik, giving the devil the name he is known by in the district. "And he is the rascal who knows how to light a fire much better than how to put it out!"

And at that reply everyone looked to try and find the smoke on the top of the donjon. In the end most of them affirmed they could distinguish it perfectly, although it was quite invisible at that distance.

The effect produced by this singular phenomenon exceeded everything imaginable. It is necessary to insist on this point. The reader must put himself in the place of the people of Werst and he will not be astonished at what follows. I do not ask him to believe in the supernatural, but to understand that this ignorant people believed in it without reservation. To the mistrust inspired by the Castle of the Carpathians, which up to then was supposed to be deserted, was to be added the terror that it now seemed to be inhabited, and by such beings! Good heavens!

There was at Werst a meeting-place frequented by drinkers, and even beloved by those who, without drinking, delighted in talking over matters at the close of the day—the latter in small numbers, be it understood. This place, open to all, was the chief, or rather the only, inn in the village.

Who was the proprietor of this inn? A Jew of the name of Jonas, a fine fellow of about sixty, of pleasing physiognomy, although rather Semitic, with black eyes, hook nose, long lip, smooth hair, and the traditional beard. Obsequious and obliging, he willingly lent little sums to one or the other without being too particular as to security nor too usurious as regards interest, although he expected to be paid on the dates fixed by the borrower. Would to heaven that the Jews in Transylvania were always as accommodating as the innkeeper of Werst!

Unfortunately this excellent Jonas was an exception. His fellows in religion, his brethren by profession—for they are all innkeepers, selling drinks and groceries—carry on the trade of money-lenders with a bitterness that is not promising for the future of the Roumanian peasant. Gradually the land is passing from the native to the foreigner. In default of being repaid their advances, the Jews are becoming the proprietors of the finest farms mortgaged to their advantage; and if the Promised Land is not to be that of Israel, it may one day make its appearance on the maps of Transylvanian geography.

The inn of the "King Mathias"—such is its name—occupies one of the corners of the terrace which crosses the main street of Werst, and is immediately opposite the biro's house. It is an old structure, half wood, half stone, much patched in places, but a good deal covered with verdure, and of very attractive appearance. It consists only of the ground floor, with a glass door giving access to the terrace. Inside one first entered a large room furnished with tables for the glasses and benches for the drinkers, with a sideboard in varnished oak on which gleamed the dishes, pots, and bottles, and a counter of black wood, behind which Jonas stood ready for his customers.

Light was obtained from two windows which were in the wall facing the terrace, and two others opposite each other in the outer walls. Of these, one was veiled by a thick curtain of climbing and hanging plants, which screened the outer view and only allowed a little light to pass, while the other when opened gave an extensive view over the lower valley of the Vulkan. A few feet below it rolled the tumultuous waters of the Nyad torrent. On one side the torrent descended the slopes of the range from its rise on the plateau of Orgall, which was crowned by the castle buildings; on the other, abundantly fed by the mountain streams, even during summer time it flowed along to the Wallachian Syl, which absorbed it in its course.

On the right, adjoining the large room, a half-dozen of small rooms were enough to accommodate the few travellers who before crossing the frontier desired to rest at the "King Mathias." They were sure of a good welcome at moderate charges, from an attentive and obliging landlord, who was always well provided with good tobacco, which he bought in the best "trafiks" of the neighbourhood. As for Jonas himself, he occupied a narrow attic, the old-fashioned window of which patched the thatch with flowers, and looked out on to the terrace.

In this inn, on this very night of the 29th of May, there were gathered all the wise-heads of Werst—Master Koltz, Magister Hermod, the forester Nic Deck, a dozen of the chief inhabitants, and also the shepherd Frik, who was not the least important of these personages. Doctor Patak was absent from this meeting of notables. Sent for in all haste by one of his old patients who was only waiting for him in order to pass away into another world, he had agreed to come to the inn as soon as his attentions were no longer necessary to the defunct.

While waiting for the doctor the company talked about the serious event of the day, but they did not talk without eating or drinking. To the hungry Jonas offered that kind of hasty pudding or maize pudding known under the name of "mamaliga," which is not at all disagreeable when taken with new milk. To the others he offered many a small glass of those strong liqueurs which roll like pure water down Roumanian throats, or "schnapps," costing about a farthing a glass, and more particularly "rakiou," a strong spirit from plums, of which the consumption is considerable among the Carpathians.

It should be mentioned that the landlord Jonas—it was the custom of the inn—only served the customers when they were sitting down, as he had observed that seated consumers consume more copiously than consumers on their feet. This evening matters looked promising, for all the seats were full; and Jonas was going from one table to another, jug in hand, filling up the glasses which were constantly empty.

It was half-past eight in the evening. They had been talking since dusk without deciding what they should do. But they were agreed on one point, and that was that if the Castle of the Carpathians was inhabited by the unknown, it had become as dangerous to Werst as a powder magazine would be at the gate of a town.

"It is very serious," said Master Koltz.

"Very serious," repeated the Magister, between two puffs of his inseparable pipe.

"Very serious," repeated the assistant.

"And no doubt," said Jonas, "that the evil repute of the castle does much harm to the country round about—"

"And now," said Magister Hermod, "there is this thing also—"

"Strangers do not come here often," said Master Koltz with a sigh.

"And now they will not come at all!" added Jonas, sighing in unison with the biro.

"Some of the people will be going away," said one of the drinkers.

"I shall go first of all," said a peasant from the outskirts; "and I will go as soon as I can sell my vines."

"For which you will find no buyers, old man," said the tavern-keeper.

One can see what these worthies were driving at in their talk. Amid the personal terrors occasioned them by the Castle of the Carpathians, rose the anxiety for their interests so regrettably injured. If there were no more travellers, Jonas would suffer in the revenue of his inn. If there were no more strangers, Master Koltz would suffer in the receipt of the tolls, which gradually grew less. If there were no more buyers, the owners could not sell their lands even at a low price. That would last for years, and the situation, already very unsatisfactory, would become worse.

In fact, if it had been so while the spirits of the castle had kept out of sight, what would it be now that they manifested their presence by material acts?

Then the shepherd Frik thought he ought to say one thing, but in a hesitating sort of way,—

"Perhaps we may have to—"

"What?" asked Master Koltz.

"Go there, master, and see."

The company looked at each other, and then lowered their eyes, and the question remained without reply.

Then Jonas, addressing Master Koltz, took up the word in a firm voice.

"Your shepherd," he said, "has just pointed out the only thing we can do."

"Go to the castle?"

"Yes, my good friends," said the innkeeper. "If there is a smoke from the donjon chimney, it is because there is a fire, and if there is a fire it must have been lighted by a hand—"

"A hand!—at least a claw!" said an old peasant, shaking his head.

"Hand or claw," said the innkeeper, "what does it matter? We must know what it means. It is the first time that smoke has come out of the castle chimneys since Baron Rodolphe of Gortz left it."

"But there might have been smoke without anybody noticing it," said Master Koltz.

"That I will never admit!" said Magister Hermod suddenly.

"But it might be," replied the biro, "if we had not got the telescope to watch what was happening at the castle."

It was well said. The phenomenon might have happened frequently and escaped even the shepherd Frik, good as were his eyes. But anyhow, whether the said phenomenon were recent or not, it was certain that human beings were actually living at the Castle of the Carpathians; and this fact constituted an extremely disturbing state of things for the inhabitants of Vulkan and Werst.

Then Magister Hermod made this remark in support of his belief,—

"Human beings, my friends? You will allow me not to believe it. Why should human beings think of taking refuge in the castle? for what reason? and how did they get there?"

"What do you think these intruders are, then?" exclaimed Master Koltz.

"Supernatural beings!" said Magister Hermod in an imposing voice. "Why should they not be spirits, goblins, perhaps even those dangerous lamias which present themselves under the form of beautiful women?"

During this enumeration every look was directed towards the door, towards the windows, or towards the chimney of the big saloon of the "King Mathias." And in truth the company asked themselves if they were not about to see one or other of these phantoms successively evoked by the schoolmaster.

"However, my good friends," said Jonas, "if these beings are of that kind, I don't understand why they should have lighted a fire, for they have no cooking to do—"

"And their sorceries?" said the shepherd. "Do you forget that they want a fire for their sorceries?"

"Evidently!" said the Magister in a tone which admitted of no reply.

The reply was accepted without protest, and in the opinion of all there could be no doubt that it must be supernatural and not human beings who had chosen the Castle of the Carpathians as the scene of their operations.

Up to this point Nic Deck had taken no part in the conversation. He had been content to listen attentively to what was said by one and the other. The old castle with its mysterious walls, its ancient origin, its feudal appearance, had always inspired him with as much curiosity as respect. And being very brave, although he was as credulous as any inhabitant of Werst, he had more than once even manifested a desire to enter the old stronghold.

As may be imagined, Miriota had obstinately set her face against so adventurous a project. He might have such ideas when he was free to do as he liked, but an engaged man was no longer his own master, and to embark in such adventures was the act of a madman, not of a lover. But notwithstanding her prayers, the lovely girl was always afraid that the forester would make some such attempt. What reassured her a little was that Nic Deck had not formally declared that he would go to the castle, for no one had sufficient influence over him to stop him—not even herself. She knew him to be an obstinate, resolute man, who would never go back on his promise. If he said a thing, the thing was as good as done. And Miriota would have been all anxiety had she suspected what the young man was thinking about.

However, as Nic Deck said nothing, the shepherd's proposition received no reply. Visit the Castle of the Carpathians now that it was haunted? Who would be mad enough to do that? And all those present discovered the best reasons for not doing anything. The biro was no longer of an age to venture over so rough a road. The magister had to look after his school. Jonas had to look after his inn. Frik had his sheep to attend to; and the other peasants had to busy themselves with their cattle and their pastures.

No! not one would venture, all of them saying to themselves,—

"He who dares go to the castle may never come back!"

At this moment the door suddenly opened to the great alarm of the company.

It was only Doctor Patak, and it would have been difficult to mistake him for one of those bewitching lamias of whom Magister Hermod had been speaking.

His patient being dead—which did honour to his medical acumen, if not to his talent—Doctor Patak had hurried on to the meeting at the "King Mathias."

"Here he is at last!" said Master Koltz.

Doctor Patak hastily shook hands with everybody, much as if he were distributing drugs, and, in a somewhat ironical tone, remarked,—

"Then, my friends, it is the castle, the Castle of the Chort, you are busy about! Oh! you cowards. But if the old castle wants to smoke, let it smoke! Does not our learned Hermod smoke, and smoke all day? Really, the whole country is in a state of terror! I have heard of nothing else during my visits. Somebody has returned and made a fire over there! And why not, if they have got a cold in the head? It would seem that it freezes in the month of May in the rooms of the donjon, unless there is some bread cooking for the other world. I suppose they want food in that place—that is if they come to life again? Perhaps they are some of the heavenly bakers who have come to start their oven."

And so on in a series of jests that were much to the distaste of the Werst people, who made no attempt to stop him.

At last the biro asked,—

"And so, doctor, you attach no importance to, what is taking place at the castle?"

"None, Master Koltz."

"Have you never said you are ready to go there—if any one dared you to do so?"

"I?" answered the doctor, with a certain look of annoyance at anyone reminding him of his words.

"Yes. Have you not said so more than once?" asked the magister.

"I have said so, certainly, and there is no need to repeat it."

"But there is need to do it!" said Hermod.

"To do it?"

"Yes; and instead of daring you, we are content to ask you to do it," added Master Koltz.

"You understand—my friends, certainly—such a proposal—"

"Well, since you hesitate," said the innkeeper, we will not ask you—we dare you!"

"Dare me?"

"Yes, doctor."

"Jonas," said the biro, "you are going too far. There is no need to dare Patak. We know he is a man of his word. What he has said he will do—if only to render a service to the village and to the whole country."

"But is this serious? You want me to go to the Castle of the Carpathians?" said the doctor, whose red face had become quite pale.

"You cannot get out of it," said Master Koltz.

"I beg you, my good friends—I beg you to be reasonable, if you please."

"We are reasonable," said Jonas.

"Be just, then. What is the use of my going there? What shall I find? A few good fellows have taken refuge in the castle, who are doing no harm to any one—"

"Well," replied Magister Hermod, "if they are good fellows you have nothing to fear from them, and it will be an opportunity for you to offer them your services."

"If they need them," said Doctor Patak, "if they send for me, I should not hesitate to go to the castle. But I do not go without an invitation, and I do not pay visits for nothing."

"We will pay you," said Master Koltz, "and at so much an hour."

"Who will pay me?"

"I will—we will—at any rate you like!" replied the majority of Jonas's customers.

Evidently, in spite of his bluster, the doctor was as big a coward as the rest of Werst. But after having posed as a superior person, after having ridiculed the popular legends, he found it difficult to refuse the service he was asked to render. But to go to the Castle of the Carpathians, even if he were paid for his journey, was in no way agreeable to him. He therefore endeavoured to show that the visit would produce no result, that the village was covering itself with ridicule in sending him to explore the castle—but his arguments hung fire.

"Look here, doctor," said Magister Hermod, "it seems to me you have absolutely nothing to fear. You do not believe in spirits?"

"No; I do not believe in them."

"Well, then, if they are not spirits who have returned to the castle, they are human beings who have taken up their quarters there, and you can get on all right with them."

The schoolmaster's reasoning was logical enough; it was difficult to get out of it.

"Agreed, Hermod," said the doctor; "but I might be detained at the castle."

"Then you will be welcomed there", said Jonas.

"Certainly; but if my absence is prolonged, and if some one in the village wants me—"

"We are all wonderfully well," said Master Koltz, "and there is not a single invalid in Werst now your last patient has taken his departure for the other world."

"Speak frankly," said the innkeeper. "Will you go?"

"No, I will not!" said the doctor. "Oh! it is not because I am afraid. You know I have no faith in these sorceries. The truth is, it seems to me absurd, and, I repeat, ridiculous. Because a smoke has appeared at the donjon chimney—a smoke which may not be a smoke—certainly not! I will not go to the Castle of the Carpathians."

"I will go!"

It was the forester Nic Deck who had suddenly joined in the conversation.

"You, Nic?" exclaimed Master Koltz.

"I—but on condition that Patak goes with me."

This was a direct thrust for the doctor, who gave a jump as if to avoid it.

"You think that, forester?" said he, "I—to go with you? Certainly. It will be a pleasant expedition for both of us, if it is of any use. Look here, Nic, you know well enough there is no road to the castle. We shall not get there."

"I have said I will go to the castle," replied Nic Deck, "and as I have said so I will go."

"But I have not said so!" exclaimed the doctor, struggling as if some one had gripped him by the collar.

"But you have!" said Jonas.

"Yes! yes!" replied the company unanimously.

The doctor, pressed on all sides, did not know how to escape. Ah! how much he regretted that he had so imprudently committed himself by his rodomontades.

Never had he imagined they would have been taken seriously, or that he would have to account for them in person. And now there was no chance of escape without becoming the laughing-stock of Werst; and in all the Vulkan district they would badger him unmercifully. He decided to accept the inevitable with a good grace.

"Well, since you wish it," he said, "I will go with Nic Deck, although it will be useless."

"Well done, Patak!" shouted all the company at the "King Mathias."

"And when shall we start, forester?" asked Doctor Patak, affecting to speak in a tone of indifference which poorly disguised his poltroonery.

"To-morrow morning," said Nic Deck.

These last words were followed by a long silence which showed how real were the feelings of Master Koltz and the others. The glasses were empty, so were the pots, but no one rose, no one thought of leaving the place although it was late, nor of returning home. It occurred to Jonas that there was a good opportunity for serving another round of schnapps and rakiou.

Suddenly a voice was heard distinctly amid the general silence, and these words were slowly pronounced,—

"Nicolas Deck, do not go to the castle to-morrow! Do not go there, or misfortune will happen to you."

Who was it said this? Whence came the voice which no one knew, and which seemed to come from an invisible mouth? It could not be a voice from a phantom, a supernatural voice, a voice from another world.

Terror was at its height. The men dared not look at one another; they dared not even utter a word.

The bravest—and that evidently was Nic Deck—endeavoured to discover what it all meant. It was evident that the words had been uttered in the room. The forester went up to the box and opened it.

Nobody.

He then looked into the rooms which opened into the saloon.

Nobody.

He opened the door, went outside, ran along the terrace to the main street of Werst.

Nobody.

A few minutes afterwards Master Koltz, Magister Hermod, Doctor Patak, Nic Deck, Shepherd Frik, and the others had left the inn and its keeper Jonas, who hastened to double-lock the door.

That night, as if they had been menaced by some apparition, the inhabitants of Werst strongly barricaded themselves in their houses.

Terror reigned in the village.

CHAPTER V.

In the morning Nic Deck and Doctor Patak prepared to start at nine o'clock. The forester's intention was to ascend the Vulkan and take the shortest way to the suspicious castle.

After the phenomenon of the smoke on the donjon, after the phenomenon of the voice heard in the saloon of the "King Mathias," we need not be astonished at the people being as if deranged. Some of the Tsiganes already spoke of leaving the district. During the night nothing else had been spoken of at home—and in a low voice. Could there be any doubt that it was the Chort who had spoken in so threatening a way to the young forester? At Jonas's inn there had been about fifty people, and these the most worthy of belief, who had all heard the strange words. To suppose that they had all been duped by some illusion of the senses was inadmissible. There could be no doubt that Nic Deck had been formally warned that misfortune would overtake him if he persisted in his intention of visiting the Castle of the Carpathians.

And yet the young forester was preparing to leave Werst, and without being forced to do so. In fact, whatever advantage Master Koltz might gain in clearing up the mystery of the castle, whatever interest the village might have in knowing what was taking place, a powerful effort had been made to get Nic Deck to go back on his word. Weeping and in despair, with her beautiful eyes wet with tears, Miriota had besought him not to persist in this adventure. After the warning given by the voice it was a serious matter; it was a mad adventure. On the eve of his marriage Nic Deck was about to risk his life in the attempt, and his betrothed clung to his knees to prevent him, but all in vain.

Neither the objurgations of his friends, nor the tears of Miriota had any effect on the young forester.

And no one was surprised at it. They knew his indomitable character, his tenacity, his obstinacy, if you will. He had said he would go to the Castle of the Carpathians, and nothing would stop him; not even the threat which had been addressed straight to him. Yes! he would go to the castle even if he never returned.

When the hour of parting came, Nic Deck pressed Miriota for the last time to his heart, while the poor girl made the sign of the thumb and two first fingers, according to Roumanian custom, which is an emblem of the Holy Trinity.

And Doctor Patak? Well, Doctor Patak had tried to get out of it, but without success. All that could be said he had said. All the objections imaginable he had mentioned. He tried to entrench himself behind the formal injunction not to go to the castle, which had been so distinctly heard.

"That menace only concerns me," said Nic Deck.

"But if anything happens to you, forester," said Doctor Patak, "shall I get away without injury?"

"Injury or not, you have promised to come with me to the castle, and you will come because I am going."

Seeing that nothing would prevent his keeping his promise, the people of Werst had resolved to help the forester. It was better that Nic Deck should not enter alone on this affair. And, much to his disgust, the doctor, feeling that he could not go back, that it would compromise his position in the village, that it would be a disgrace for him to go back after all his boastings, resigned himself to the adventure with terror in his soul, and fully resolved to profit by the least obstacle on the road to make his companion turn back.

Nic Deck and Doctor Patak set out, and Master Koltz, Magister Hermod, Frik, and Jonas accompanied them up to a turning out of the main road, where they stopped.

Here Master Koltz for the last time brought his telescope—which he was never without—to bear on the castle. There was now no smoke from the donjon chimney, and it would have been easy to see it on the clear horizon of a beautiful spring morning. Were they to conclude that the guests, natural or supernatural, of the castle had vanished on finding that the forester took no heed of their threats? Some of them thought so, and therein appeared a decisive reason for bringing the adventure to a satisfactory termination. And so they all shook hands, and Nic Deck, dragging the doctor away with him, disappeared round the hill.

The young forester was in full visiting costume, laced cap with large peak, belted vest with a cutlass in its sheath, baggy trousers, iron-shod boots, cartridge-belt at his waist, and long gun on his shoulder. He had the deserved reputation of being a first-rate shot, and in default of ghosts it was as well to be prepared for robbers, or even bears with evil intentions.

The doctor had armed himself with an old flint pistol, which missed fire three times out of five. He also carried a hatchet which his companion had given him in case it was necessary to cut a way through the thick underwoods of Plesa. He wore a large country hat, and was buttoned up in a thick travelling cape, and shod with big iron-soled boots; but this heavy costume would not have stopped him from running away if opportunity presented itself.

Both he and Nic Deck carried a few provisions in their wallets, so as to prolong the exploration if necessary.

After leaving the by-road, Nic Deck and the doctor went along the right bank of the Nyad for a few hundred yards. Had they followed the road which winds through the valleys, they would have gone too far to the westward. It was a pity they could not follow the river and thereby reduce their distance by a third, for the Nyad rises in the folds of the Orgall plateau. But though it was practicable at first, the bank became eventually so deeply cut into by ravines and barred with rocks that progress along it was impossible even to pedestrians. They had therefore to bear away obliquely to the left, so as to return to the castle after traversing the lower belt of the Plesa forests.

And this was the only side on which the castle was approachable from where they were. When it had been inhabited by Count Rodolphe de Gortz, the communication between the village of Werst, the Vulkan Hill, and the valley of the Syl had been through a gap which had been opened in this direction. But abandoned for twenty years to the invasions of vegetation, it had become obstructed by an inextricable thicket of underwood, and the trace of a footpath or a passage would be sought for in vain.

When they left the deep bed of the Nyad, which was filled with roaring water, Nic Deck stopped to take his bearings. The castle was no longer visible. It would only appear again beyond the curtain of forests which stood in rows one above the other on the lower slopes of the mountain, an arrangement common to the whole orographic system of the Carpathians. As there was no landmark the direction was not easily made out. It could only be arrived at from the position of the sun, whose rays were lighting up the distant crests in the south-west.

"You see, forester," said the doctor, "you see there is not even a road, or, rather, no more road."

"There will be one," said Nic Deck.

"That is easy to say, Nic."

"And easy to do, Patak."

"You are resolved, then?"

The forester was content to reply by an affirmative gesture, and started off towards the trees.

The doctor had a strong inclination to retrace his steps, but his companion, happening to turn round, gave him such a determined look that he thought it better not to remain behind.

Doctor Patak then conceived another hope: Nic Deck might get lost amid this labyrinth of woods, where his duties had not yet called him. But he reckoned without that marvellous scent, that professional instinct, that animal aptitude, so to speak, which takes notice of the least indications, projections of branches in such and such directions, irregularities of the ground, colours of the bark, hues of the mosses as they are exposed to different winds. Nic Deck was a perfect master of his trade, and practised it with too much sagacity to go astray even in localities unknown to him. He was worthy to be ranked with Leatherstocking or Chingachgook in the land of Cooper.

But the crossing of this zone of trees was not free from real difficulties. Elms, beeches, a few of those maples known as false planes, mighty oaks, occupied the first line up to the line of the birches, pines, and spruces, massed on the higher shoulders of the col to the left. Magnificent were these trees with their powerful stems, their boughs warm with the new sap, their thick leafage intermingling to form a roof of verdure which the sun's rays could not pierce.

By stooping beneath their lower branches a passage was relatively easy; but many were the obstacles on the surface of the ground, and much work was needed to clear them away, to get through the nettles and briars, to avoid the thousands of thorns that clung to them at the least touch. Nic Deck was not a man to become anxious about these matters; and, providing he got through the wood, he did not worry himself about a few scratches. The advance, however, under such conditions was necessarily slow, and that was regrettable, for Nic Deck and Doctor Patak wished to reach the castle in the afternoon, in order that they might return to Werst before night.

Hatchet in hand, the forester worked at clearing a passage through these thick thorn-bushes, bristling with vegetable bayonets, in which the foot met a rugged soil, hummocky, broken, with roots or stumps to stumble over when it did not sink in a swampy bed of dead leaves which the wind had never swept away. Myriads of pods shot off like fulminating peas to the great alarm of the doctor, who started back at the crackle, and came again when some twig would catch on to his vest like a claw that wished to keep him. No! poor man, he was not at all comfortable. But now he dared not return alone, and he had to make an effort to keep up with his intractable companion.

Occasionally capricious clearings appeared in the forest. A shower of light would penetrate it. A couple of black storks, disturbed in their solitude, escaped from the higher branches and flew off with powerful strokes of the wing. The crossing of these clearings made the advance still more fatiguing. In them were piled up enormous masses of trees blown down by the storm or fallen from old age, as if the axe of the wood man had given them their death-stroke. There lay enormous trunks eaten into with decay, which no tool would ever cut into billets, and no waggon would ever carry to the bed of the Wallachian Syl. Faced by these obstacles, which were difficult to clear and at times impossible to turn, Nic Deck and his companion had no easy time of it. If the young forester, active, supple, vigorous, managed well, the doctor with his short legs, his large corporation, breathless and exhausted, could not save himself from occasional falls, and Nic had to come to his assistance.

"You will see, Nic, that I shall end by breaking one of my limbs!" he said.

"You will soon patch it up, if you do."

"Come, forester, be reasonable; we need not strive against the impossible!"

But Nic Deck was already on in front, and the doctor, obtaining no reply, hastened to rejoin him.

Were they in the right direction to come out in front of the castle? They would have been puzzled to prove it. But as the ground was on the rise all the time, they must be reaching the edge of the forest; and they arrived there at three o'clock in the afternoon.

Beyond, up to the plateau of Orgall extended the curtain of green trees, much more scattered the farther they were up the mountain.

The Nyad appeared among the rocks, either because it had curved to the north-west, or because Nic Deck had struck off obliquely towards it. The young forester was thus assured he had made a good course, for the brook took its rise in the Orgall plateau.

Nic Deck could not refuse the doctor an hour's rest on the bank of the torrent. Besides, the stomach claimed its due as well as the limbs. The wallets were well furnished; rakiou filled the doctor's flask as well as Nic's. Besides, water, fresh and limpid, filtered amid the pebbles below, and flowed a few paces off. What more could they desire? They had lost much; they must repair the loss.

Since their departure the doctor had scarcely had the leisure to talk with Nic Deck, who had been in front of him all the time. But he made up for lost time when they were seated on the bank of the Nyad. If one was not talkative, the other fully made up for it; and we need not be astonished if the questions were prolix and the answers brief.

"Let us talk a little, forester, and talk seriously," said the doctor.

"I am listening to you," replied Nic Deck.

"I think we halted here to recover our strength?"

"Nothing could be more correct."

"Before returning to Werst?"

"No; before going to the castle."

"But, Nic, we have been walking for six hours, and we are hardly halfway."

"That shows we have no time to lose."

"But we shall not reach the castle before night, and as I imagine, forester, you will not be mad enough to run any risks until you have had a clear view of it, we shall have to wait for day light."

"We will wait for daylight."

"And so you will not give up this project, which has no common sense in it?"

"No."

"What! Here we are exhausted, wanting a good table in a good room, and a good bed in a good room, and you are going to pass the night in the open air?"

"Yes! if any obstacle prevents us from penetrating into the castle."

"And if there is no obstacle?"

"We will sleep in the rooms in the donjon."

"The rooms in the donjon!" exclaimed Doctor Patak. "Do you think, forester, that I shall ever consent to spend a whole night inside that cursed castle?"

"Certainly, unless you prefer to stay outside alone."

"Alone, forester! That was not in the bargain; and if we are to separate, I would rather start at once and go back to the village."

"It was in the bargain that you would follow me into the castle."

"In the day, yes! In the night, no!"

"Well, you can go if you like; but take care you do not get lost in the thickets."

Lost! That was what troubled the doctor. Abandoned to himself, unaccustomed to these interminable circuits in the Plesa forests, he felt he was incapable of finding the way back to Werst. Besides, to be alone when night fell— a very dark night, perhaps—to descend the slopes of the hill at the risk of collapsing in the bottom of a ravine, that certainly was not agreeable to him. He was freed from having to enter the castle when the sun was down, and if the forester persisted, he had better follow him up to the enclosure. But the doctor made a last effort to stop his companion.

"You know well, my dear Nic," he continued, "that I will never consent to separate from you. If you persist in going to the castle, I will not allow you to go there alone."

"Well spoken, Doctor Patak, and I think you ought to stick to that."

"No! One word more, Nic. If it is night when we arrive, promise me not to try and enter the castle."

"What I promise you, doctor, is not to go back one footstep until I have discovered what is going on there."

"What is going on there, forester!" said Doctor Patak, shrugging his shoulders. "But what do you want to go on there?"

"I know nothing, and as I have made up my mind to know, I will know."

"But shall we ever reach this devil's castle?" asked the doctor, whose arguments were exhausted. "To judge by the difficulty we have had up to now, and the time it has taken us to get through the Plesa forests, the day will end before we are in sight of the wall."

"I do not think so," said Nic Deck. "In the higher ranges the pines have no such thickets as do the elms or maples or beeches."

"But the ground is rough."

"What does that matter, if it is not impracticable?"

"But I believe that bears are met with on the outskirts of the plateau."

"I have my gun, and you have your pistol to defend yourself with, doctor."

"But if night falls we may be lost in the darkness."

"No; for we now have a guide, which guide will, I hope, not leave us any more."

"A guide?" exclaimed the doctor. And he rose abruptly to cast an anxious look around him.

"Yes," said Nic, "and this guide is the Nyad. We have only to go up the right bank to reach the very crest of the plateau where it takes its source. I think we shall be at the castle gate in two hours, if we get on the road without delay."

"In two hours if not in six!" replied the doctor.

"Are you ready?"

"Already? Nic, already? Why, our halt has only lasted a few minutes—"

"A few minutes which make a good half-hour. For the last time, are you ready? "

"Ready—when my legs are like lumps of lead? You know well enough, Nic Deck, my legs are not forester's legs. My feet are swollen in my boots, and it is cruel to make me follow you—"

"Ah! You annoy me, Patak! You can go back alone if you like! Pleasant journey to you!"

And Nic rose.

"For the love of God, forester," cried Doctor Patak, "listen to me."

"Listen to your foolery?"

"It is already late, why not remain here? why not encamp under the shelter of these trees? We can start at daylight, and have all the morning to reach the plateau."

"Doctor," replied Nic Deck, "I tell you again it is my intention to spend the night in the castle."

"No!" cried the doctor.; "no, you shall not do it, Nic! I will stop you—"

"You?"

"I will cling to you! I will drag you back! I will thrash you, if necessary!"

The unfortunate doctor did not know what he was saying.

As to Nic Deck, he did not even reply. Putting his arm through the gun-strap, he started to go up the Nyad.

"Wait—wait!" cried the doctor piteously. "What a fiend of a man! One moment! My limbs are stiff, my joints will not work."

But they soon had to work, for the doctor had to trot along on his little legs to catch up the forester, who never looked back.

It was four o'clock. The solar rays just tipped the crest of Plesa, which intercepted them, and by an oblique reflection lighted up the higher branches of the pine-forest. Nic Deck had cause to hurry, for the woods below were growing dark at the decline of day.

Of a different character were the higher forests, which consisted mainly of the commoner Alpine species. Instead of being deformed and twisted and gnarled, the stems were straight and upright and far apart, and bare of branches for fifty or sixty feet from their roots, and then their evergreen verdure spread out like a roof. There was little brushwood or entanglement at their base; but the long roots crept along the ground as if they were snakes grown torpid with the cold. The ground was carpeted with close yellowish moss, scattered over with dry twigs, and dotted with cones which crackled under the feet. The slope was rough and furrowed with crystalline rocks, the sharp edges of which made themselves felt through the thickest leather. For a quarter of a mile the passage through the pine-wood was difficult. To climb these blocks required a suppleness, a vigour, and a sureness of foot which Doctor Patak could no longer claim. Nic Deck would have got through in an hour if he had been alone but it took him three with the hindrance of his companion, whom he had to stop to attend to, and to help over rocks too high for his little legs. The doctor had but one fear—a terrible fear—that of being left alone in these gloomy solitudes.

However, if the slopes became more painful to climb, the trees began to get thinner and thinner on the Plesa ridge. They were now in isolated clumps and of small size. Between these clumps could be seen the ranges of mountains in the background, with their outline still traceable in the evening mist.

The torrent of the Nyad, which the forester had continued to follow, was now not larger than a brook, and rose not so very far off. A few hundred feet above the last folds of the ground lay the rounded plateau of Orgall, crowned by the castle buildings.

Nic Deck at length reached the plateau after a final effort which reduced the doctor to the state of an inert mass. The poor man had not strength to drag himself twenty yards farther, and he fell like the ox before the axe of the butcher.

Nic Deck hardly felt the fatigue of this painful ascent. Erect, motionless, he devoured with his gaze this Castle of the Carpathians he had never before been so near.

Before his eyes lay a crenellated wall defended by a deep ditch, the only drawbridge of which was drawn up against a gate surrounded by a ring of stone.

Around the wall, on the plateau, all was bare and silent.

In the twilight the mass of castle buildings was confusedly distinguishable. There was no one visible on either wall or donjon, nor on the circular terrace. Not a trace of smoke curled round the vane.

"Well, forester," said Doctor Patak, "are you convinced that it is possible to cross the ditch, lower the drawbridge, and open the gate?"

Nic Deck did not reply. He saw that it would be necessary to halt before the castle walls. Amid the darkness, how could he descend into the ditch and climb the slope so as to enter the wall? Evidently the best thing to do was to wait for the coming dawn, and work in broad daylight.

And that was what it was decided to do, to the great annoyance of the forester and the extreme satisfaction of the doctor.

CHAPTER VI.

The thin crescent of the moon, like a silver sickle, disappeared almost as soon as the sun set. A few clouds rising in the west, soon extinguished the last gleams of twilight. Darkness gradually rose from below and covered all. The ring of mountains was blotted out in obscurity, and the castle soon disappeared beneath the pall of night.

If the night promised to be very dark, there was nothing to indicate that it would be troubled by any atmospheric disturbance, rain or storm; and this was fortunate for Nic Deck and his companion, who were about to encamp in the open air.

There was no clump of trees on this barren plateau of Orgall. Here and there were a few shrubs, which afforded no shelter against the nocturnal cold. There were rocks in plenty, some half-buried in the ground, others in such a state of equilibrium that the slightest push would have sent them rolling down into the fir-woods.

The only plant that grew in profusion on the rocky soil was the thistle known as Russian thorn, whose seeds, says Elisée Reclus, were carried in their coats by the Muscovite horses—"a present of cheerful conquest which the Russians gave the Transylvanians."

A search was made for a more comfortable place in which to pass the night, and which would afford some shelter against the fall in temperature which is remarkable in these altitudes.

"We have more than chances enough—to be miserable!" murmured Doctor Patak.

"Are you not satisfied, then?" asked Nic Deck.

"Certainly not! What a splendid place to catch a good cold or the rheumatism, which I do not know how I shall ever get cured of!"

A very artless confession on the part of the old quarantine officer. How he regretted his comfortable little house at Werst, with its room so snug and its bed so well furnished with pillows and counterpane!

Among the stones on the Orgall plateau one had to be selected whose position offered the best shelter against the south-west wind, which was beginning to freshen. This was what Nic Deck did, and soon the doctor joined him behind a large rock which was as flat as a table on its upper surface.

This stone was one of those stone benches amid the scabiouses and saxifrages which are frequently met with at the turnings of the road in Wallachia. While the traveller sits on them he can quench his thirst with the water contained in a vase placed on them, and which is every day renewed by the country people. When Baron Rodolphe de Gortz lived at the castle, this bench bore a bowl which the family servants never left empty. But now it was dirty and worn and covered with green mosses, and the least shock would have reduced it to dust.

At the end of the seat rose a granite shaft, the remains of an ancient cross, nothing being left of the arms, although a half-effaced groove showed where they had been.

Doctor Patak, being a strong-minded man, was unable to admit that this cross could protect him against supernatural apparitions. But by an anomaly common to a good many of the incredulous, although he did not believe in God, he was not very far from believing in the devil. In his heart he believed the Chort was not far off; he it was that haunted the castle, and neither the closed gate, the raised drawbridge, the lofty wall, nor the deep ditch would keep him from coming out, if the fancy took him, to come and twist both their necks.

And when the doctor saw that he had to spend a whole night under these conditions, he shuddered with terror. No! It was too much to require of a human creature, and it would be more than the most energetic of characters could bear.

And then an idea came to him tardily—an idea he had not thought of before he left Werst. It was Thursday evening, and on that day the people of the district, the country people, were careful not to go out after sundown. Thursday they knew to be a day of evil deeds. Their legends told them that if they ventured abroad on that day, they ran the risk of meeting with some evil spirit. And so no one moved about on the roads and by-ways after nightfall.

And here was Doctor Patak not only away from home, but close to a haunted castle, two or three miles from the village. And here he would have to stop until the dawn came—if it ever came again! In truth, this was simply tempting the devil!

Deep in these thoughts, the doctor saw the forester carefully take out of his bag a piece of cold meat, after having a good drink from his flask. The best thing, it occurred to him, was to do likewise, and he did so. A leg of a goose, a thick slice of bread, the whole well moistened with rakiou, was the least he could take to revive his strength. But if that calmed his hunger, it did not calm his fears.

"Now let us sleep," said Nic Deck, as soon as he had put his bag at the foot of the stone.

"Sleep, forester?"

"Good-night, doctor."

"Good-night—that is easy to wish, but I am afraid it will not end well."

Nic Deck, being in no humour for conversation, made no reply. Accustomed by his vocation to sleep amid the woods, he threw himself down close to the stone seat and was soon in a deep sleep. And the doctor could but grumble between his teeth when he heard his companion breathing at regular intervals.

As for him, it was impossible for him for some minutes to deaden his senses of hearing and seeing. In spite of his fatigue he continued to see and to listen. His brain was a prey to those extravagant visions which are due to the troubles of insomnia.

What was he looking for in the depths of darkness?—the hazy shapes of the objects which surrounded him, the scattered clouds across the sky, the almost imperceptible mass of the castle? The rocks on the Orgall plateau seemed to be moving in a sort of infernal saraband. And if they were to crumble on their bases, slip down the slope, roll on to the two adventurers, and crush them at the castle gate to which admission was denied them!

The unhappy doctor got up; he listened to the noises which are ever present on lofty table-lands—those disquieting murmurs which seem to whisper and groan and sigh. He heard the nyctalops fanning the rocks with frenzied wing, the stryges in their nocturnal flight, and two or three pairs of funereal owls whose hooting echoed like a cry of pain. Then his muscles contracted all at once, and his body trembled, bathed in icy perspiration.

In this way the long hours went by until midnight. If the doctor had been able to talk, to exchange but a few words now and then, to give free course to his recriminations, he would have been less afraid. But Nic Deck slept and slept in a deep slumber.

Midnight—that terrible hour for all, the hour of apparitions, the hour of evil deeds!

What could it be?

The doctor had just got up again. He was asking himself if he were awake, or if he were suffering from a nightmare.

Overhead he thought he saw—no! he really did see the strangest of shapes, lighted by a spectral light, pass from one horizon to the other, rise, fall, and drift down with the clouds. They looked like monsters, dragons with serpents' tails, hippogryphs with huge wings, gigantic krakens, enormous vampires, fighting to seize him in their claws or swallow him in their jaws.

Then everything appeared to be in motion on the Orgall plateau—the rocks, the trees at its edge. And very distinctly a clanging at short intervals reached his ear.

"The bell!" he murmured, "the castle bell!"

Yes! It was indeed the bell of the old chapel, and not that of the church at Vulkan, which the wind would have borne in the opposite direction.

And now the strokes became more hurried. The hand that struck no longer tolled a funeral knell. No! It was an alarm, whose urgent strokes were awaking the echoes of the Transylvanian frontier.

As he listened to these dismal vibrations, Doctor Patak was seized with a convulsive fear, an insurmountable anguish, an irresistible terror which thrilled his whole body with cold shudderings.

But the forester had been awakened by the alarming clanging of the bell. He rose while Doctor Patak seemed as if beside himself.

Nic Deck listened, and his eyes tried to pierce the deep darkness which overhung the castle.

"That bell! That bell!" repeated Doctor Patak. "It is the Chort that is ringing it!"

Decidedly the poor terrified doctor was thinking more than ever of the devil.

The forester remained motionless, and did not reply. Suddenly a series of roars as if from some huge animal at a harbour's mouth broke forth in tumultuous undulations.

For a long distance around the air resounded with this deafening growl.

Then a light darted from the centre of the donjon, an intense light, from which leapt flashes of penetrating clearness and blinding coruscations. From what could come this powerful light, the irradiations of which spread in long sheets over the Orgall plateau? From what furnace came this photogenic stream, which seemed to embrace the rocks at the same time as it bathed them with a strange lividity?

"Nic—Nic!" exclaimed the doctor. "Look at me! Am I a corpse like you?"

In fact they had both assumed a corpse-like look. Their faces were pallid, their eyes seemed to have gone, the orbits being apparently empty; their cheeks were greyish green, like the mosses which the legend says grow on the heads of those that are hanged.

Nic Deck was astounded at what he saw, at what he heard. Doctor Patak was in the last stage of fright; his muscles retracted, his skin bristled, his pupils dilated, his body was seized with tetanic rigidity. As the poet of the "Contemplations" remarks, "he breathed in terror."

A minute—a minute or more—lasted this terrifying phenomenon. Then the strange light gradually went out, the groaning ceased, and the Orgall plateau resumed its silence and obscurity.

Neither of the men thought any more of sleep. The doctor overwhelmed with stupor, the forester upright against the stone seat, awaited the return of the dawn.

What did Nic Deck think of these things, which were evidently so supernatural to his eyes? Were they not enough to shake his resolution? Did he still intend to pursue this reckless adventure?

Certainly he had said that he would enter the castle, that he would explore the donjon. But was it not enough for him to have come to its insurmountable wall, to have evoked the anger of its guardian spirits, and provoked this trouble of the elements? Would he be reproached with not having kept to his promise if he returned to the village without having urged his folly to the end in entering this diabolic castle?

Suddenly the doctor threw himself upon him, seized him by the hand, and strove to drag him away, saying in a hoarse voice, "Come! come!"

"No!" said Nic Deck.

And in turn he caught hold of Doctor Patak, who fell at this last effort.

At last the night ended, and such was their mental state that neither forester nor doctor knew the time that elapsed until daybreak. They remembered nothing of the hours which preceded the first rays of the morning.

At that moment a rosy streak appeared on the crest of Paring, on the eastern horizon, on the other side of the valley of the two Syls. The faint white rays of dawn dispersed over the depth of the sky, and striped it as if it were a zebra-skin.

Nic Deck turned towards the castle. He saw it grow clearer and clearer: the donjon revealed itself from the high mists which came floating down the Vulkan slope; the chapel, the galleries, the outer walls emerged from the nocturnal mists; and there on the corner bastion appeared the beech-tree, with its leaves rustling in the easterly breeze.

There was no change in the ordinary aspect of the castle. The bell was as motionless as the old feudal weather-vane. No smoke arose from the donjon chimneys, and the barred windows remained obstinately closed.

Above the platform, in the higher zones of the sky, a few birds were flying and gently calling to each other.

Nic Deck turned to look at the principal entrance to the castle. The drawbridge up against the bay closed the postern between the two stone pillars which bore the arms of the barons of Gortz.

Had the forester resolved to continue this adventurous expedition to the end? Yes; and his resolution had not been shaken by the events of the night. A thing said was a thing done—that was his motto as we know. Neither the mysterious voice which had threatened him personally in the saloon of the "King Mathias," nor the inexplicable phenomenon of sound and light he had just witnessed, would stop him from entering the castle. An hour would be enough for him to hurry through the galleries, visit the keep, and then, having fulfilled his promise, he would return to Werst, where he would arrive during the morning.

As to Doctor Patak, he was now only an inert machine, without either the strength to resist or to insist. He would go where he was driven. If he fell, it would be impossible to lift him again. The terrors of the night had reduced him to complete imbecility, and he made no observation when the forester pointed to the castle and said,—

"Come on!"

And yet the day had returned, and the doctor could have got back to Werst without fear of losing himself in the Plesa forests. He had no reason to wish to remain with Nic Deck, and if he did not abandon his companion to return to the village, it was that he was no longer conscious of the state of affairs, and was merely a body without a mind. And so when the forester dragged him towards the slope of the counterscarp he made no resistance.

But was it possible to enter the castle otherwise than by the gate? That was what Nic Deck endeavoured to discover.

The wall showed no breach, no falling in, no excavation, giving access to the interior. It was indeed surprising that these old walls were in such a state of preservation, but this was doubtless due to their thickness. To climb to the line of crenellations which crowned them appeared to be impracticable, as they rose some forty feet above the ditch. And it seemed as though Nic Deck, at the very moment of reaching the Castle of the Carpathians, was to fail owing to insurmountable obstacles.

Fortunately—or very unfortunately for him—there stood above the postern a sort of loophole, or rather an embrasure, through which formerly pointed the muzzle of a culverin. By making use of one of the chains of the drawbridge which hung down to the ground, it would not be very difficult for an active, vigorous man to hoist himself up to this embrasure. Its width was sufficient to allow of a man to pass, unless it was barred on the inside, and Nic Deck could probably manage to get through it within the castle wall.

The forester saw at once that this was the only way open to him, and that is why, followed by the unconscious doctor, he went obliquely down the inner slope of the counterscarp.

They were soon at the bottom of the ditch, which was strewn with stones amid the thickets of wild plants. They could hardly find a place to step, and they were not sure that myriads of venomous beasts did not swarm in the herbage of this humid excavation.

In the middle of the ditch, and parallel to the wall, was the ancient trench, now nearly dry, which they could just stride across.

Nic Deck, having lost nothing of his mental or bodily energy, went on coolly and quietly, while the doctor followed him mechanically, like an animal at the end of a string.

After crossing the trench, the forester went along the base of the curtain for some twenty yards, and stopped underneath the gate close to one end of the chain of the drawbridge. By the help of his hands and feet he could thence easily reach the line of stonework that jutted out just below the embrasure.

Evidently Nic did not intend to compel the doctor to take part with him in this escalade. So heavy a man could not have clone so. He therefore contented himself with giving him a vigorous shake to make him understand, and then advised him to wait without moving at the bottom of the ditch.

Then Nic Deck commenced to climb the chain; and this was merely child's play for his mountaineer's muscles.

But when the doctor found himself alone, the true position of things, to a certain extent, recurred to him. He understood, he looked, he saw his companion already suspended a dozen feet from the ground, and in a voice choking with the bitterness of fear, he cried,—

"Stop—Nic—stop!"

The forester heard him not.

"Come—come—or I will go away!" cried the doctor.

"Go, then," said Nic.

And he continued to raise himself along the chain of the drawbridge.

Doctor Patak, in a paroxysm of terror, would have gone back again up the slope of the counterscarp, so as to reach the crest of the Orgall plateau and return full speed to Werst.

But—prodigy to which the wonders of the preceding night were as nothing— he could not move. His feet were held fast as if they had been seized in the jaws of a vice. Could he place one before the other? No. They stuck by the heels and soles of his boots. Had the doctor been taken in a trap? He was too much frightened to look, but it seemed as though he was held by the nails in his boots.

Whatever it was, the poor man was immovable. He was fixed to the ground. Not having strength to cry out, he stretched out his hands in despair. It looked as though he sought to be rescued from the embrace of some tarask hidden in the bowels of the earth.

Meanwhile Nic Deck had got as high as the postern, and was placing his hand on the ironwork in which the hinges of the drawbridge were embedded.

A cry of pain escaped him; then throwing himself back, as if he had been struck by lightning, he slipped along the chain, which a final instinct made him clutch, and rolled to the bottom of the ditch.

"The voice truly said that misfortune would come to me," he murmured, and then he lost consciousness.

CHAPTER VII.

How can we describe the anxiety to which the village of Werst had been a prey since the departure of the young forester and Doctor Patak? And it had constantly increased as the hours elapsed, and seemed interminable.

Master Koltz, the innkeeper Jonas, Magister Hermod, and a few others had remained all the time on the terrace, each of them keeping a constant watch on the distant castle to see if any wreath of smoke appeared over the donjon. No smoke showed itself—as was ascertained by means of the telescope, which was incessantly brought to bear in that direction. Assuredly the two florins sunk in the acquisition of that instrument had been well invested. Never had the biro, although so much interested in the matter, betrayed the slightest regret at so opportune an expenditure.

At half-past twelve, when the shepherd Frik returned from the pasture, he was eagerly interrogated. Was there anything new, anything extraordinary, anything supernatural?

Frik replied that he had just come along the valley of the Wallachian Syl without seeing anything suspicious.

After dinner, about two o'clock, the people went back to their post of observation. No one dreamt of remaining at home, and no one would certainly have dreamt of setting foot within the grand saloon of the "King Mathias," where comminatory voices made themselves heard. That walls have ears is all very well, it is a popular proverb but a mouth!

And so the worthy innkeeper might well fear that his inn had been put into quarantine, and consequently his anxiety was extreme. Would he have to shut up shop, and drink his own stock for want of customers? And with a view of restoring confidence among the people of Werst, he had undertaken a lengthy search throughout the "King Mathias:" he had searched the rooms, under the beds, explored the cupboards and the sideboard, and every corner of the large saloon, the cellar, and the store-room, from which any ill-disposed practical joker might have worked the mystification.

Nothing could he find, not even along the side of the house overlooking the Nyad. The windows were too high for it to be possible for anyone to climb to them along a perpendicular wall, the foundation of which went sheer down into the impetuous torrent. It mattered not! Fear does not reason, and considerable time would doubtless elapse before Jonas's habitual guests would return to their confidence in his inn, his schnapps, and his rakiou.

Considerable time? That is a mistake, and, as we shall see, this gloomy prognostic was never realized.

In fact, a few days later, in a quite unexpected way, the village notables were to resume their daily conferences, varied with refreshments, in the saloon of the "King Mathias."

But we must first return to the young forester and his companion, Doctor Patak.

It will be remembered that when he left Werst, Nic Deck had promised the disconsolate Miriota that he would make his visit to the Castle of the Carpathians as brief as possible. If no harm happened to him, if the threats fulminated against him were not realized, he expected to get back early in the evening. He was therefore waited for, and with what impatience! Neither the girl, nor her father, nor the schoolmaster could foresee that the difficulties of the road would prevent the forester from reaching the crest of the Orgall plateau before nightfall.

And, in consequence, the anxiety, which had been intense during the day, exceeded all bounds when eight o'clock struck in the Vulkan clock, which could be heard distinctly at Werst. What could have happened to prevent both Nic and the doctor from returning after a day's absence? Nobody thought of going home before they came back. Every minute they were seen in imagination corning round some turning in the road or along some gap in the hills.

Master Koltz and his daughter had gone to the end of the road, where the shepherd had been placed on the lookout. Many times they thought they saw somebody in the distance through the clearings among the trees. A pure illusion! The hillside was deserted, as usual, for it was not often that the frontier folk ventured there at night. And it was Thursday evening—the Thursday of evil spirits—and on that day the Transylvanian never willingly stirs abroad after sundown. It seemed that Nic Deck must have been mad to have chosen such a day for his visit to the castle; the truth being that the young forester had not given it a thought, as indeed had no one else in the village.

But Miriota was thinking a good deal about it now. And what terrible imaginings occurred to her! In imagination she had followed her lover hour by hour, through the thick forests of the Plesa as he made his way up to the Orgall plateau. And now that night had come she seemed to see him within the wall, endeavouring to escape from the spirits which haunted the Castle of the Carpathians. He had become the sport of their malevolence. He was the victim devoted to their vengeance. He was imprisoned in the depths of some subterranean gaol—dead, perhaps.

Poor girl, what would she not have given to throw herself on his track! And as she could not do that, at least she could wait all night in this place. But her father insisted on her going home, and, leaving the shepherd on the watch, returned with her to his house.

As soon as she was in her little room Miriota abandoned herself to tears. She loved him with all her heart, this brave Nic, and with a love all the more grateful owing to the young forester not having sought her under the conditions on which marriages are generally arranged in these Transylvanian countries.

Every year, at the feast of St. Peter, there opens "the fair of the betrothed." On that day all the marriageable girls of the district are assembled. They come in their best carriages drawn by their best horses; they bring with them their dowry, that is to say, the clothes they have spun, and sewn, and embroidered with their hands, and these are all packed in gaudily coloured boxes; their relatives and women friends and neighbours accompanying them. And then the young men arrive dressed in their best clothes and girt with silken sashes; proudly they strut through the fair; they choose the girl they take a fancy to, they give her a ring and a handkerchief in token of betrothal, and the marriages take place at the close of the fair.

But it was not in one Of these marriage fairs that Nic Deck had met Miriota. Their acquaintanceship had not come about by chance. They had known each other from childhood; they had loved as soon as they were old enough to love.

The young forester had not had to seek her out at a sale. But why was Nic Deck of so resolute a character? why was he so obstinate in keeping an imprudent promise? And yet he loved her, although she had not enough influence over him to stop his going to this wretched castle.

What a night the sorrowful Miriota had amid her terrors and her tears! She could not sleep. Stooping at her window, looking out on the rising road, she seemed to hear a voice that whispered,—

"Nicolas Deck has defied the warning. Miriota has no longer a lover."

But that was but a mistake of her troubled senses. No voice came across the silence of the night. The phenomenon of the saloon of the "King Mathias" was not reproduced in the house of Master Koltz.

At dawn next morning the population of Werst were astir. From the terrace to the rise of the hill, some went one way, some another, along the main road—some asking for news, some giving it. They said that Frik the shepherd had gone off about a quarter of a mile from the village, not to enter the forest, but to skirt it, and that he had some reason for doing so.

The people were waiting for him, and in order to communicate more promptly with him, Master Koltz, Miriota, and Jonas went to the end of the village.

Half an hour afterwards Frik was observed a few hundred yards away up the rising road.

As he did not appear to be in a hurry, good news was not expected.

"Well, Frik," said Master Koltz as soon as the shepherd came up, "what have you discovered?"

"I have seen nothing and discovered nothing," said Frik.

"Nothing!" murmured the girl, whose eyes filled with tears.

"At daybreak," continued the shepherd, "I saw two men about half a mile away. At first I thought it was Nic Deck accompanied by the doctor, but it was not."

"Do you know who the men were?" asked Jonas.

"Two travellers who had crossed the frontier in the morning."

"You spoke to them?"

"Yes."

"Were they coming towards the village?"

"No; they were going towards Retyezat, bound for the summit."

"Two tourists?"

"They looked like it, Master Koltz."

"And as they crossed the Vulkan during the night, they saw nothing near the castle?"

"No—for they were then on the other side of the frontier," replied Frik.

"Have you no news of Nic Deck?"

"None."

There was a sigh from poor Miriota.

"Besides," said Frik, "you can have a talk to these travellers in a day or two, for they are thinking of staying at Werst before setting out for Kolosvar."

"Provided some one does not speak evil of my inn!" thought Jonas. "They would never care to stay there!"

For the last thirty-six hours the excellent landlord had been possessed by this fear that no traveller dare henceforth eat and sleep at the "King Mathias."

In short, these questions and answers between the shepherd and his master had in no way cleared matters up. And as neither the young forester nor Doctor Patak had reappeared by eight o'clock in the morning, could it be reasonably hoped that they would ever reappear? The Castle of the Carpathians was not to be approached with impunity.

Crushed by the emotions of that sleepless night, Miriota could bear up no longer. She almost fainted away, and hardly had strength to walk. Her father took her home. There her tears redoubled. She called Nic in a heartrending voice. She would have gone out to find him. And all pitied her and feared she was going to have a serious illness.

However, it was necessary and urgent to do something. Some one ought to go to the help of the forester and the doctor without losing a moment. That he would have to run into danger, ill exposing himself to the attack of the beings, human or otherwise, who occupied the castle, mattered little. The important thing was to know what had become of Nic and the doctor. This duty fell not only to their friends, but to every inhabitant of the village. The bravest could not refuse to cross the Plesa forests and ascend to the Castle of the Carpathians.

That was decided after many discussions. The bravest were found to consist of three: these were Master Koltz, the shepherd Frik, and the innkeeper Jonas— not one more. As for Magister Hermod he was suddenly seized with gout in the leg, and had to stretch himself out on two chairs while he taught in his school.

About nine o'clock Master Koltz and his companions, well-armed in case of eventualities, took the road to the Vulkan. And at the very turning where Nic Deck had left it, they left it to plunge into the woods.

In fact they said to themselves, not without reason, that if the young forester and the doctor were on their way back to the village, this was the road by which they would come; and it would be easy to get on their track once the three were through the outer line of trees.

We will leave them, to relate what happened at Werst as soon as they were out of sight. If it had appeared indispensable that volunteers should go off to the rescue of Nic Deck and Patak, it was considered to be unreasonably imprudent now that they were gone. It would be a fine conclusion if the first catastrophe were to be doubled by a second! That the forester and the doctor had been the victims of their attempt, no one doubted; and what was the use of Master Koltz and Frik and Jonas exposing themselves to another disaster? They would indeed be getting on when the girl had to weep for her father as she had to weep for her betrothed; when the friends of the shepherd and the inn keeper had to reproach themselves with their loss!

The grief became general at Werst, and there was no sign that it would soon end. Even supposing that no harm happened to them, the return of Master Koltz and his two companions could not be reckoned upon before night had fallen on the heights of the Plesa.

What, then, was the surprise when they were sighted about two o'clock in the afternoon some distance along the road! With what eagerness did Miriota, who was at once told of their approach, run to meet them!

There were not three, there were four; and the fourth appeared in the shape of the doctor.

"Nic—my poor Nic!" exclaimed the girl, "Nic is not there?"

Yes—Nic Deck was there, stretched on a litter of boughs, which Jonas and the shepherd bore with difficulty.

Miriota rushed towards her betrothed, she stooped over him, she clasped him in her arms.

"He is dead!" she exclaimed, "he is dead!"

"No, he is not dead," replied Doctor Patak, "but he deserves to be—and so do I!"

The truth is, the forester was unconscious. His limbs were stiff, his face bloodless, his respiration hardly moved his chest. As for the doctor, his face was not as colourless as his companion's, owing to the walk having restored his usual brick-red tint.

Miriota's voice, so tender, so heartrending, could not awake Nic Deck from the torpor in which he was plunged. When he had been brought into the village and laid in a room in Master Koltz's house, he had not uttered a word. A few moments afterwards, however, his eyes opened, and when he saw the girl stooping over him, a smile played on his lips; but when he tried to raise himself he could not. A part of his body was paralyzed as if he had been struck with hemiplegia. At the same time, wishing to comfort Miriota, he said to her—in a very feeble voice, it is true,—

"It will be nothing, it will be nothing."

"Nic—my poor Nic!" said the girl.

"A little over-fatigue, dear Miriota, and a little excitement. It will be over soon, with your nursing."

But the patient required calm and repose; and so Master Koltz went away, leaving Miriota near the young forester, who could not have wished for a more attentive nurse, and soon fell asleep.

Meanwhile, the innkeeper Jonas related to a numerous audience, and in a loud voice so as to be heard by all, what had happened after their departure.

Master Koltz, the shepherd, and himself, after finding the footpath cut by Nic Deck and the doctor, had gone on towards the Castle of the Carpathians. For two hours they made their way up the Plesa slopes, and the edge of the forest was not more than half a mile off, when two men appeared. These were the doctor and the forester, one quite helpless in his legs, the other just about to fall at the foot of a tree, owing to exhaustion.

To run to the doctor; to interrogate him, but without being able to obtain a single word, for he was too stupefied to reply; to make a litter with the branches, to lay Nic Deck on it, to put Patak on his feet,—did not take very long. Then Master Koltz and the shepherd, who relieved Jonas from time to time, resumed the road to Werst.

As to saying why Nic Deck was in such a state, and if he had entered the ruins of the castle, the innkeeper knew no more than Master Koltz or the shepherd Frik, and the doctor had not yet sufficiently recovered his spirits to satisfy their curiosity.

But if Patak had not yet spoken, it was necessary for him to speak now. He was in safety in the village, surrounded by his friends, and in the midst of his patients. He had nothing to fear from the things at the castle. And even if they had wrung from him an oath to be silent, to say nothing of what he had seen at the Castle of the Carpathians, the public interest required that he should ignore that oath.

"Compose yourself, doctor," said Master Koltz, "and try and remember."

"You wish me to speak?"

"In the name of the inhabitants of Werst, and for the sake of the safety of the village, I order you to do so."

A large glass of rakiou, brought in by Jonas, had the effect of restoring to the doctor the use of his tongue, and in broken sentences he expressed himself in these terms:—

"We went off, both of us, Nic and I. Fools, fools! It took nearly all day to get through those wretched forests. We did not get up to the castle before it was getting dark. I still tremble at it—I will tremble at it all my life. Nic wanted to go in. Yes! He wanted to spend the night in the donjon, as much as to say to sleep in the bedroom of Beelzebub."

Doctor Patak said these things in a voice so cavernous that all who heard him shuddered.

"I did not consent!" he continued; "no, I did not consent. And what would have happened if I had yielded to Nic Deck's desires? My hair stands on end to think of it."

And if the doctor's hair did not stand on end, it was because his hand wandered mechanically over his poll.

"Nic accordingly resigned himself to camping on the Orgall plateau. What a night! my friends, what a night! Try to rest when the spirits will not let you sleep an hour—no, not even one hour. Suddenly fiery monsters appeared in the clouds, regular balauris! They hurled themselves on to the plateau to devour us."

Every look was turned towards the sky, to make sure that a few spectres were not there in full gallop.

"And a few moments after," continued the doctor, " the chapel bell began to clang!"

Every ear was stretched towards the horizon, and more than one of the crowd believed they could hear the distant ringing in the direction of the castle, so much had the doctor's recital impressed his audience.

"Suddenly," he went on, "fearful bellowings filled the air, or rather the roaring of wild beasts. Then a bright light darted from the windows of the donjon. An infernal flame illumined all the plateau up to the fir forest. Nic Deck and I looked at one another. Ah! the terrible vision! We were like two corpses— two corpses which the lurid light set making horrible grimaces at each other."

And to look at Doctor Patak, with his convulsed face and his wild eyes, there really would have been some excuse for asking if he had not returned from that other world whither he had already sent so many of his kind.

He had to be left to recover his breath, for he was incapable of continuing his story. This cost Jonas a second glass of rakiou, which appeared to bring back to the doctor some portion of the senses which the other spirits had made him lose.

"But what happened to poor Nic Deck?" asked Master Koltz.

And, not without reason, the biro attached extreme importance to the doctor's reply, for it was the young forester who had been personally threatened by the voice of the spirits in the saloon of the "King Mathias."

"As far as I remember," continued the doctor, "the daylight returned. I besought Nic Deck to abandon his projects. But you know him—he could not be more obstinate if he would. He went down into the ditch, and I was forced to follow him, for he dragged me along with him. Besides, I really do not know what I did. Nic went on up to the gate. He caught hold of the chain of the draw bridge, with which he pulled himself up the wall. At this moment the sense of our position occurred. There was still time to stop him, that rash—I say more— that sacrilegious young man. For the last time I ordered him to come down, to come back on the road to Werst. 'No!' he shouted to me. I would have run away— yes, my friends, I confess it—I would have fled, and there is not one of you who would not have had the same thought in my place! But it was in vain I tried to move from the ground. My feet were nailed, screwed, rooted. I tried to free them—it was impossible. I tried to struggle—it was useless!"

And Doctor Patak imitated the desperate movements of a man held by the legs, as a fox is held in a trap. Then, resuming his story, he said,—

"At this moment there was a cry—and such a cry! It was Nic Deck who uttered it. His hands had let go the chain, and he fell to the bottom of the ditch as if he had been struck by an invisible hand."

The doctor, it is clear, had told what had happened, and his imagination had added nothing, excited though it might be. Just as he had described them, so had the prodigies appeared of which the Orgall plateau had been the scene during the preceding night.

What had happened after Nic Deck's fall was as follows—The forester had fainted, and Doctor Patak was incapable of helping him, for his boots were stuck to the ground, and he could not get his swollen feet out of them. Suddenly the invisible force that detained him vanished. His legs were free. He rushed towards his companion, and, what must be considered a noble act of courage, he bathed Nic Deck's face with his handkerchief, which he dipped in the water of the stream. The forester recovered consciousness, but his left arm and a part of his body were helpless after the frightful shock he had had. However, with the doctor's aid he managed to get up and climb the slope of the counterscarp and regain the plateau. Then he set out for the village. After an hour's progress the pain in his arm and side became so violent that he had to stop. And it was just as the doctor was about to start off alone in search of help from Werst, that Master Koltz and Jonas and Frik arrived most opportunely.

The doctor carefully avoided saying that the young forester had been seriously hurt, although he was generally very positive when consulted on medical matters.

"When the ailment is a natural ailment," he said in a dogmatic tone, "it is serious. But when we have to deal with a supernatural ailment sent by the Chort, it is only the Chort who can cure it."

In default of a diagnosis it cannot be said that this prognosis was reassuring for Nic Deck. There have, however, been many physicians since Hippocrates and Galen who have made mistakes, and these have been far better men than Doctor Patak. The young forester was a healthy lad; with his vigorous constitution there was reason to hope that without any diabolic intervention he would recover, on condition that he was not too careful to accept the advice of the old quarantine officer.

CHAPTER VIII.

Such things were not calculated to calm the terrors of the people of Werst. There could now be no doubt that the threats uttered by the "mouth of darkness," as the poet said in the "King Mathias," were to be taken seriously. Nic Deck, struck in this inexplicable manner, had been punished for his disobedience and temerity. Was not this a warning to all those who might be tempted to follow his example? Here, clearly enough, was a formal prohibition against entering the Castle of the Carpathians. Whoever tried it would risk his life. Most certainly if the forester had got within the wall he would never have returned to the village.

And so the fright was more complete than ever at Werst, and even at Vulkan, and also throughout the valley of the two Syls. Nothing less was spoken of than leaving the district, and a few gipsy families moved off rather than live in the vicinity of the castle. That it should be a refuge for supernatural and maleficent beings was more than the popular feeling could put up with. The only thing to do was to go into some other part of the country, unless the Hungarian Government decided to destroy this inaccessible haunt. But was the Castle of the Carpathians destructible by the only means man had at his disposal?

During the first week of June no one would venture out of the village, not even to work in the fields. Might not the least stroke of a spade provoke the apparition of some phantom buried in the ground? The coulter of the plough as it cut the furrow, might it not set in flight a flock of staffii or stryges? Where the seed of corn was sown, might not the seed of demons spring up?

"That could not fail to happen!" said the shepherd Frik in a tone of conviction.

And, as far as he was concerned, he took good care not to return with his sheep to the pastures of the Syl.

And so the village was in a state of terror. No one went to work in the fields. Everyone remained at home with doors and windows closed. Master Koltz did not know what to do to restore confidence among those under his rule. Evidently the only way was to go to Kolosvar and invoke the intervention of the authorities.

And had the smoke reappeared at the top of the donjon chimney? Yes; many times the telescope had made it visible among the mists which swept the Orgall plateau.

And when night came, had the clouds assumed a rosy hue as if from the reflection of a fire? Yes; and it was said that fiery plumes could be seen curling and whirling over the castle.

And that roaring which had frightened Doctor Patak, was it heard from among the woods of Plesa, to the terror of the people of Werst? Yes; or at least, notwithstanding the distance, the north-west wind brought along fearful growlings which were augmented by the echoes of the hills.

According to some of the more terror-stricken, the ground was shaken by subterranean tremblings as if some ancient volcano had become active again in the Carpathian chain. But possibly there was a good deal of exaggeration in what the Werstians thought they saw and heard and felt. Under any circumstances there were positive, tangible reasons, it will be admitted, why living in such a strangely troubled country was no longer possible.

The "King Mathias" remained deserted in consequence. A lazaretto in an epidemic could not have been more shunned. No one had the audacity to cross the threshold, and Jonas was asking himself if for want of customers he would not have to retire from trade, when the arrival of two travellers altered matters considerably.

In the evening of the month of June, about eight o'clock, the latch of the door was lifted from the outside; but the door, being bolted inside, could not be opened.

Jonas, who had already retired to his attic, hastily came down. To the hope of finding himself face to face with a customer was added the fear that the customer might be some evil-looking ghost, to whom he would be only too ready to refuse board and lodging.

Jonas proceeded to hold a parley through the door without opening it.

"Who is there?" he asked.

"Two travellers."

"Alive?"

"Very much alive."

"Are you sure of it?"

"As much alive as we can be, Mr. Innkeeper; but we shall die of hunger if you keep us outside."

Jonas decided to drawback the bolts, and two men entered the room.

As soon as they were in, their first demand was for a room each, as they intended to stay a day at Werst.

By the light of the lamp Jonas examined the newcomers with great attention, and made sure that he had really to deal with human beings. How fortunate for the "King Mathias"!

The younger of the travellers might be about thirty-two years old, of tall stature, with a noble, handsome face, black eyes, dark-brown hair, a well-cut brown beard, a somewhat sad but proud look about him—in fact he was a gentleman, and an experienced innkeeper like Jonas could not be mistaken in such a matter.

Besides, when he asked what names he was to enter in his visitors' book, the younger man replied,-

"The Count Franz de Télek and his man Rotzko."

"Of what place?"

"Krajowa."

Krajowa is one of the chief towns of the State of Roumania, which borders the Transylvanian provinces south of the Carpathian chain.

Franz de Télek was thus of Roumanian nationality, as Jonas had seen from the very first.

Rotzko was a man of about forty, solidly built and strong, with a thick moustache, bristly hair, and quite a military bearing. He carried a soldier's knapsack strapped to his shoulders, and a valise small enough to be carried in his hand.

That was all the baggage of the young count, who travelled generally on foot, as could be seen from his costume—a cloak in a roll over his shoulder, a light cap on his head, a short jacket with a belt, from which hung the leather sheath of the Wallachian knife, and he wore the gaiters strapped down to the broad, thick-soled shoes.

These travellers were the two whom the shepherd Frik had met twelve days before on the road to the hills, when they were going to Retyezat. After seeing the country up to Maros, and making the ascent of the mountain, they had come for a little rest to Werst before exploring the valley of the two Syls.

"You have two rooms we can have?" asked Franz de Télek.

"Two—three—four—as many as the count pleases," said Jonas.

"Two will do," said Rotzko, "but they must be near each other."

"Will these suit you?" asked Jonas, opening two doors at the end of the large saloon.

"Very well indeed," said Franz de Télek.

Evidently Jonas had nothing to fear from his new customers. These were no supernatural beings, no phantoms who had assumed the shape of men. No! This gentleman was one of those personages of distinction whom an innkeeper is always honoured in welcoming, and who might perhaps bring the "King Mathias" into fashion again.

"How far are we from Kolosvar?" asked the count

"About fifty miles, if you go by the road through Petroseny and Karlsburg," replied Jonas.

"Is it a tiring sort of walk?"

"Yes, very tiring for walkers; and if I may be permitted to say so, the count would seem to require a rest of a few days before undertaking it—"

"Can we have anything to eat?" asked Franz de Télek, cutting short the innkeeper's remarks.

"In half an hour's time I shall have the honour of offering the count a repast worthy of him."

"Bread, wine, eggs, and cold meat will be enough for to-night."

"I will go and see about them."

"As soon as possible."

"This moment."

And Jonas was hurrying off to the kitchen when a question stopped him.—

"You do not seem to have many people at your inn?" said Franz de Télek.

"No—not just at the moment, sir."

"Is not this the time for people to come and have a drink and smoke a pipe?"

"It is too late now, sir. They go to bed with the chickens in the village of Werst."

Never would he have said why the "King Mathias" was without a customer.

"Are there not three or four hundred people in this village?"

"About that, sir."

"Why did we not meet a living soul as we came down the main street?"

"That is because—to-day—well, it is Saturday, you see—and the day before Sunday is—"

Franz de Télek did not persist, luckily for Jonas, who did not know what to reply. Nothing in the world would have induced him to reveal the true state of affairs. Strangers would learn that only too soon, and who could tell if they would not hasten to leave a village so deservedly suspected?

"It is to be hoped that that voice will not begin to chatter in the big room while they are at supper!" thought Jonas as he laid the table.

A few minutes afterwards the very simple meal ordered by the young count was neatly served on a clean white cloth. Franz de Télek sat down, and Rotzko seated himself facing him, as they usually did on their travels. Both of them ate with a good appetite; and when the repast was over they retired to their rooms.

As the young count and Rotzko had hardly spoken ten words during their meal, Jonas had not been able to take part in their conversation—to his great displeasure. Besides, Franz de Télek did not seem to be communicative. As to Rotzko, the innkeeper, after due survey, gathered that he would not be able to get anything out of him regarding his master's family.

Jonas had, therefore, to content himself with bidding his visitors good-night. Before he went up to his attic he gave a good look around the room, and lent an anxious ear to the least noises within and without, saying to himself,—

"May that abominable voice not awake them from their sleep!"

The night passed tranquilly.

At daybreak next morning the news began to spread in the village that two travellers had arrived at the "King Mathias," and a number of people gathered in front of the inn.

Franz de Télek and Rotzko were still sleeping, tired after their excursion the day before. There was little likelihood of their rising before seven or eight o'clock. And consequently there was great impatience among the spectators, who had none of them the courage to enter the room before the travellers.

At eight o'clock they came in together. Nothing regrettable had happened. They could be seen walking about in the inn. Then they sat down to breakfast. All of which was particularly reassuring.

Jonas stood at the front door and smiled amiably, inviting his old customers to give him another trial. The traveller who honoured the "King Mathias" with his presence was a gentleman—a Roumanian gentleman, if you please, and of one of the oldest Roumanian families what was to be feared in such noble company?

In short, it happened that Master Koltz, thinking it his duty to set an example, took the risk of the first step.

About nine o'clock the biro entered the room in rather a hesitating way. Almost immediately he was followed by Magister Hermod and three or four other customers, as well as the shepherd Frik. As to Doctor Patak, it had been impossible to persuade him to accompany them.

"Set foot again in Jonas's!" he said. "Never, until he pays me two florins a visit."

We may here remark, as it is a matter of some importance, that if Master Koltz had consented to return to the "King Mathias," it was not solely with a view of satisfying his curiosity, nor with the intention of making the acquaintance of Count Franz de Télek, No! self-interest was his chief motive.

As a traveller the young count had become liable for a tax on self and man, and it must not be forgotten that these taxes went direct into the pocket of the chief magistrate of Werst.

The biro at once went forward and politely stated his demand, and Franz de Télek, although taken somewhat by surprise, immediately settled the claim.

He even begged the biro and the schoolmaster to be seated for a moment at his table, and the offer was so politely made that they could not refuse.

Jonas hastened to serve them with drinks, the best he had in his cellar, and then a few of the natives of Werst asked for a drink on their own account, and it seemed as though the old customers, for a moment dispersed, would soon be as plentiful as ever in the "King Mathias."

Having paid the traveller's tax, Franz de Télek wished to know if it were productive.

"Not as much as we wish," replied Master Koltz.

"Do strangers only come here occasionally then?"

"Very occasionally," said the biro, "and yet the country is worth a visit."

"So I think," said the count. "What I have seen appeared to me to be well worth a traveller's attention. From the top of the Retyezat I much admired the valley of the Syls, the villages away to the east, and the range of mountains which closes in the view."

"It is very fine, sir, very fine! " said Magister Hermod; "and to complete your tour you should make the ascent of Paring."

"I am afraid I shall not have the necessary time," said the count.

"One day would be enough."

"Probably; but I am going to Karlsburg, and I must start to-morrow morning."

"What!" said Jonas with his most amiable air. "Does the count think of leaving us so soon?"

And he would not have been sorry if the visitors could have stayed some time at the "King Mathias."

"It must be so," said the Count de Télek, "Besides, what would be the use of my making a longer stay at Werst?"

"Believe me, our village is well worth a tourist's making some stay at," said Master Koltz.

"But it does not seem to be much frequented," said the count, "and that is probably because its neighbourhood has nothing remarkable about it."

"Quite so—nothing remarkable," said the biro, thinking of the castle.

"No—nothing remarkable," said the schoolmaster.

"Oh! ah!" said the shepherd Frik, the exclamation escaping involuntarily.

What looks he received from Master Koltz and the others, particularly from the innkeeper!

Was it then advisable to let the stranger into the secrets of the district? Should they reveal to him what had passed on the plateau of Orgall, and direct his attention to the Castle of the Carpathians? Would that not frighten him and make him anxious to leave the village? And in the future what travellers would come by the Vulkan road into Transylvania?

Truly the shepherd had shown no more intelligence than if he were one of his own sheep.

"Be quiet, you imbecile, be quiet!" said Master Koltz to him in a whisper.

But as the young count's curiosity had been awakened, he addressed himself directly to Frik, and asked him what he meant by his "Oh! ah!"

The shepherd was not a man to retreat, and perhaps really thought that Franz de Télek might give some advice which the village might profitably adopt.

"I said, 'Oh, ah!'" replied the shepherd, "and I will not go back on my word."

"Is there any marvel, then, to visit in the neighbourhood of Werst?"

"Any marvel?" replied Master Koltz.

"No! no!" exclaimed the bystanders. And they were already in fear at the thought lest a fresh attempt at entering the castle would bring fresh misfortunes on them.

Franz de Télek, not without some surprise, took notice of those people whose faces were expressive of alarm in all sorts of ways, but all equally unmistakable.

"What is this all about?" he asked.

"What is it, sir?" replied Rotzko. "Well, it seems there is the Castle of the Carpathians."

"The Castle of the Carpathians?"

"Yes! That is the name this shepherd has just whispered in my ear."

And as he spoke Rotzko pointed to Frik, who nodded his head without daring to look at his master.

But a breach was now made in the wall of the private life of the superstitious village, and all its history could not help going forth through this breach.

In fact, Master Koltz, who had made up his mind how to act, resolved to explain matters himself to the count, and told him all he knew about the Castle of the Carpathians.

Naturally Franz de Télek could not hide the astonishment the story caused him, nor the feelings it suggested to him. Although he knew little of scientific matters, like other young people of his class who live in their castles in these Wallachian byways, he was a sensible man. He believed but little in apparitions and laughed at legend. A castle haunted by spirits merely excited his incredulity. In his opinion, in all that Master Koltz had told him there was nothing of the marvellous, but only a few facts, more or lest proved, to which the people of Werst attributed a supernatural origin. The smoke from the donjon, the bell ringing violently, could be very easily explained, and the lightnings and roarings from within the wall might be purely imaginary.

Franz de Télek did not hesitate to say so, and to joke about it, to the great scandal of his listeners.

"But, count, there is something else," said Master Koltz.

"What is that?"

"Well, it is impossible to get into this Castle of the Carpathians."

"Indeed?"

"Our forester and our doctor tried to get in a few days ago, for the benefit of the village, and they paid dearly for their attempt."

"What happened to them?" asked Franz de Télek, somewhat ironically.

Master Koltz related in detail the adventures of Nic Deck and Doctor Patak.

"And so," said the count, "when the doctor wanted to get out of the ditch his feet were so stuck to the ground that he could not take a step forward?"

"Neither a step forward nor a step behind," added Magister Hermod.

"Your doctor thought so," replied Franz de Télek. "But it was fear which stuck him by the heels."

"Be it so," replied Master Koltz. "But Nic Deck received a frightful shock when he put his hand on the ironwork of the drawbridge."

"A terrible shock—"

"So terrible," replied the biro, "that he has been in bed ever since."

"Not in danger of his life, I hope?" said the count.

"No, fortunately."

That was a fact, an undeniable fact, and Master Koltz waited for the explanation Franz de Télek would give.

"In all I have just heard there is nothing, I repeat, but what is very simple. I have no doubt but what somebody is now living in the castle—who, I know not. Anyhow, they are not spirits, but people who wish to lie hidden there after taking refuge there—criminals probably."

"Criminals!" exclaimed Master Koltz.

"Probably; and as they do not want anyone to hunt them out, they wish it to be believed that the castle is haunted by supernatural beings."

"What!" said Magister Hermod. "You think—"

"I think you are very superstitious in these parts, that the people in the castle know it, and that they wish to keep off visitors in that way."

That this was the true explanation was not unlikely, but we need not be astonished if nobody at Werst would admit it.

The young count saw that he had in no way convinced an audience who did not wish to be convinced, and so he contented himself with adding,—

"If you do not care to agree with me, gentlemen, you can continue to think what you please about the Castle of the Carpathians."

"We believe what we have seen," replied Master Koltz.

"And what is—" said the magister.

"Well. Really, I am sorry I have not a day to spare, for Rotzko and I would have paid a visit to your famous castle, and I assure you we would soon have found out—"

"Visit the castle!" exclaimed Master Koltz.

"Without hesitation, and the devil himself would not have stopped us from getting in."

On listening to Franz de Télek express himself so positively, so ironically even, the villagers were seized with terror. In treating the spirits of the castle with such indifference, would he not bring some disaster on the village? Did not these spirits hear all that passed in the inn of the "King Mathias"? Would the voice be heard a second time in this room?

And thereupon Master Koltz told the young count of the circumstances under which the forester had been personally threatened when he decided on entering the Castle of the Carpathians.

Franz de Télek simply shrugged his shoulders; then he rose, saying that no voice had been heard in the room as they pretended. Whereupon some of the company made for the door, not caring to remain any longer in a place where a young sceptic dared say such things.

But Franz de Télek stopped them with a gesture.

"Assuredly, gentlemen," he said. "I see that the village of Werst is under the empire of fear."

"And not without reason," replied Master Koltz.

"Well, there is a very simple way of putting a stop to the performances which according to you are going on at the Castle of the Carpathians. After to-morrow I shall be at Karlsburg, and if you like I will tell the town authorities. They will send you a few police, and I will answer for it that these brave fellows will know how to get into the castle and clear out the jokers who are practising on your credulity, or arrest the scoundrels, who are perhaps preparing for some new iniquity."

Nothing could be more acceptable than this proposal, but yet it was not to the taste of the notables of Werst. In their opinion neither the police nor the army itself would succeed against these superhuman beings, who would know how to defend themselves by supernatural means.

"But I believe," continued the young count, "that you have not yet told me to whom this Castle of the Carpathians belongs or belonged?"

"To an old country family, the family of the Barons of Gortz," said Master Koltz.

"The family of Gortz!" exclaimed Franz de Télek.

"The same."

"Is that the family to which Baron Rodolphe belonged?"

"Yes."

"And do you know what has become of him?"

"No; for the baron has not come back to the castle for years."

Franz de Télek had become quite pale, and mechanically in an altered voice he repeated the name,—

"Rodolphe de Gortz!"

CHAPTER IX.

The family of the Counts of Télek was one of the most ancient and illustrious in Roumania, having been of considerable importance there before the country conquered its independence in the beginning of the sixteenth century. With all the political movements which abound in the history of these provinces the name of the family is gloriously connected.

Less favoured than the famous beech of the Castle of the Carpathians, which still possessed three branches, the house of Télek was now reduced to one, that of Télek of Krajowa, whose last offspring was the young gentleman who had just arrived at the village of Werst.

During his infancy he had never left the patrimonial castle where the Count and Countess of Télek lived. The descendants of the family were held in great esteem in the country, where they spent their wealth generously. Living the liberal, easy life of the country nobility, it was seldom that they left their estate at Krajowa more than once a year, and that when business took them to the town of that name, which was only a few miles away.

This kind of life had of necessity an influence on the education of their only son, and for long afterwards Franz felt the effects of the surroundings amid which his childhood was passed. His only tutor was an old Italian priest, who could only teach him what he knew, and he did not know much. And so when the boy had become a young man he had but a very inadequate knowledge of science or art or contemporary literature. To be an enthusiastic sportsman, afoot night and day through the forests and on the plains, hunting the stag and the wild bear, and attacking the wild beasts of the mountains, knife in hand, such were the ordinary pastimes of the young count, who, being very brave and very resolute, accomplished wonders in these rough occupations.

The Countess of Télek died when her son was scarcely fifteen, and he was only one-and-twenty when his father died in a hunting accident.

The grief of young Franz was extreme. As he had wept for his mother he wept for his father, who had just been taken from him, one after the other, within these few years. All his tender feelings, all the affectionate impulses of his heart, were then centred in this filial love which had been sufficient for him during his childhood and youth. But when this love failed him, having no friends and his tutor being dead, he found himself alone in the world.

For three years the young count remained at the Castle of Krajowa. He could not make up his mind to leave it. He lived there without seeking to make any acquaintances outside. Once or twice he had been to Bucharest, but that was because certain matters obliged him to go there; and these were but short absences, for he was in haste to return to his domain.

This life could not, however, last for ever, and Franz began to feel the want of enlarging the horizon which was so restricted by the Roumanian mountains; and he wished to fly beyond it.

The young count was about twenty-three years old when he made up his mind to travel. His wealth enabled him to fully gratify his wishes. One day he left the Castle of Krajowa to his old servants and left the Wallachian country. He took with him Rotzko, an old Roumanian soldier, who had been for ten years in the family, and who had been the young count's companion in all his hunting expeditions. He was a man of courage and resolution, entirely devoted to his master.

The young count's intention was to visit Europe and to stay a few months in the capitals and important towns of the Continent. He considered, not without cause, that his education, which had been only begun at the Castle of Krajowa, might be completed by what he learnt on a carefully planned tour.

It was to Italy that Franz de Télek wished to go first, for he could speak Italian fairly well, the old priest having taught him. The attraction of this country, so rich in memories, was such that he stayed there four years. He only left Venice to go to Florence, he left Rome but to go to Naples, constantly returning to these artistic centres, from which he could not tear himself away. France, Germany, Spain, Russia, England he would see later on; he would even study them to better advantage—so it seemed to him—when age had matured his ideas. On the other hand, he must be in all the effervescence of youth to enjoy the charms of the great Italian cities.

Franz de Télek was twenty-seven when he went to Naples for the last time. He intended to spend only a few hours there before leaving for Sicily. By the exploration of the ancient Trinacria he purposed to end his tour, and then return to his Castle of Krajowa and have a year's rest.

An unexpected circumstance not only changed his plans, but decided his life and changed its course.

During the few years he had lived in Italy the young count had not learned much of the sciences, for which he felt no aptitude, but the sense of the beautiful had been revealed to him like light to a blind man. With his mind widely opened to the splendours of art, he had become enthusiastic over the masterpieces of painting, in visiting the galleries of Naples, Rome, and Florence. At the same time the theatres had made him acquainted with the lyric works of the time, and he became powerfully interested in their interpretation by the great artistes.

It was during his last stay at Naples, and under circumstances we are about to relate, that a sentiment of a more personal character, of more intensive penetration, took possession of his heart.

There was then at the theatre of San Carlo a celebrated singer whose pure voice, finished method, and dramatic ability had won the admiration of all the dilettanti. Up to then La Stilla had never sought the applause of foreigners, and had never sung any other music than Italian, which then held the first place in the art of composition. The Carignan Theatre at Turin, the Scala at Milan, the Fenice, at Venice, the Alfieri at Florence, the Apollo at Rome, the San Carlo at Naples, introduced her in turn, and her triumphs left her no room for regret that she had not appeared at the other theatres of Europe.

La Stilla, then aged five-and-twenty, was a woman of ideal beauty, with her long golden hair, the ardour of her deep-black eyes, the purity of her complexion, and a figure which the chisel of a Praxiteles could not have made more perfect. And this woman had become a sublime artiste, another Malibran, of whom Musset could also say,— "And thy songs in the skies bore away sorrow."

But this voice which the most adored of poets has celebrated in his immortal stanzas, "that voice of the heart which only finds the heart," that voice was La Stilla's in all its inexpressible magnificence.

However, this incomparable prima donna, who reproduced with such perfection the accents of tenderness, the fury of the passions, the most powerful feelings of the soul, had never, so they said, experienced their effect. Never had she loved, never had her eyes responded to the thousand looks which were concentrated on her on the stage. It seemed that she lived but for her art and only for her art.

The first time he saw La Stilla, Franz experienced that irresistible ardour which is the essence of a first love. And he gave up his plan of leaving Italy, after visiting Sicily, and resolved to remain at Naples until the close of the season. As if some invisible bond he could not break had attached him to the singer, he was at all the performances, which the enthusiasm of the public converted into veritable triumphs. Many times, incapable of mastering his passion, he had tried to obtain access to her house; but La Stilla's door remained as pitilessly closed against him as against so many other fanatic admirers.

And so it came about that the young count became the most to be pitied of men. Always in sight of his love, thinking only of the great artiste, living but to see her and hear her, he sought no longer to make friends in the world to which his name and fortune called him.

Soon this excitement so increased with Franz that his health was in danger. We can imagine what he might have suffered if he had had to bear the tortures of jealousy, if La Stilla's heart had belonged to another. But the young count had no rival, as he knew, and none could give him umbrage—not even a certain peculiar personage, of whose appearance and character our story requires more notice.

He was a man between fifty and fifty-five at the time Franz de Télek last went to Naples. This incommunicative individual apparently strove to live outside the social conventionalities that prevail in the higher circles. Nothing was known of his family, his position, his past life. He was met with to-day at Rome, to-morrow at Florence, provided that La Stilla was at Florence or at Rome. In fact, he lived but to listen to the renowned singer, who then occupied the foremost place in the art of song.

If Franz de Télek had lived only in the delirium of his idolatry for La Stilla since the day he had applauded her, or rather had seen her on the stage at Naples, this eccentric dilettante had been following her about for six years. But he was not like the young count; in his case it was not the woman but the voice which had become so necessary to his life as the air he breathed. Never had he sought to see her except on the stage, never had he called at her house or attempted to write to her. But every time La Stilla appeared, in no matter what theatre of Italy, there passed in among the audience a man of tall stature, wrapped in a long dark overcoat, and wearing a large hat which hid his face. This man would hurry to his seat in a private box previously engaged for him, and there he would remain, silent and motionless, throughout the performance. But as soon as La Stilla had finished her last air, he would go away furtively, and no other singer would detain him—he had not even heard them.

Who was this spectator, so strangely assiduous at these performances? La Stilla had in vain sought to know; and, being of a very impressionable nature, she had become quite frightened at this curious man—an unreasonable terror, but still a very real one. Although she could not see him in the back of his box, she knew he was there, she felt his look imperiously fixed on her, and, greatly troubled by his presence, she no longer heard the cheers with which the public welcomed her appearance on the scene.

We have said that this personage had never approached La Stilla. Nothing could be truer. But if he had not tried to make her acquaintance—and we must particularly insist on this point—all that could remind him of the artiste had been the object of his constant attention. Thus he possessed the finest of the portraits which the great painter, Michel Gregorio, had made of the singer. This was, indeed, La Stilla impassioned, vibrating, sublime, incarnate in one of her finest characters, and the portrait acquired for its price in gold was well worth the price her wealthy admirer had paid for it.

If this eccentric individual was invariably alone when he occupied his box during La Stilla's performances, if he never went out of his rooms but to go to the theatre, it must not be supposed that he lived in absolute isolation. No; a companion no less eccentric shared his existence.

This individual was known as Orfanik. How old was he? whence came he? where was he born? No one could have answered those three questions. To listen to him—for he was only too glad to talk—he was one of those unrecognized geniuses who have taken an aversion to the world; and it was supposed, and not without reason, that he was some poor devil of an inventor who was chiefly supported by the purse of his protector.

Orfanik was of middle height, thin, sickly, consumptive, and pale. He was remarkable for a black patch over his right eye, which he had lost in some experiment; and on his nose was a pair of spectacles, the only lens being that over his left eye, which glowed with a greenish look. During his solitary walks, he gesticulated as if he were talking to some invisible being who listened without ever answering.

These two characters, the strange melomaniac and the no less strange Orfanik, were known, at least as much as they wished to be, in all the towns of Italy to which the theatrical season regularly took them. They had the privilege of exciting public curiosity; and although the admirer of La Stilla had always repulsed the reporters and their indiscreet interviews, they had at last discovered his name and nationality. He was of Roumanian birth, and the first time Franz de Télek asked who he was, they told him,—

"The Baron Rodolphe de Gortz."

Such was the state of affairs when the young count arrived at Naples. For two months the theatre of San Carlo had been full, and the success of La Stilla grew greater every evening. Never had she done herself more justice in her different characters, never had she called forth more enthusiastic ovations.

At each performance, while Franz occupied his orchestra stall, the Baron de Gortz sat at the back of his box, absorbed in this ideal song, impregnated with this divine voice, without which it seemed he could not live.

It was then that a rumour spread at Naples—a rumour the public refused to believe, but which eventually alarmed the dilettanti.

It was said that at the close of the season La Stilla was going to retire from the stage. What! In all the possession of her talent, in all the plenitude of her beauty, in the apogee of her artistic career, was it possible she thought of retiring?

Unlikely as it seemed, it was true, and undoubtedly the Baron de Gortz had something to do with her resolve.

This spectator with his mysterious proceedings, always there, although invisible behind the railing of his box, had at length provoked in La Stilla a nervous, persistent emotion which she could not overcome. Whenever she came on the stage she felt an influence come over her, and the excitement, which was apparent enough to the public, had gradually injured her health.

To leave Naples, to fly to Rome, to Venice, or to some other town of the peninsula, would not, she knew, deliver her from the presence of Baron de Gortz. She would not even escape him by abandoning Italy for Germany, Russia, or France. He would follow her wherever she made her self heard; and to deliver herself from this besetting importunity, her only chance was to abandon the stage.

Two months before the rumour of her retirement had been heard, Franz de Télek had taken a step with regard to the singer, the consequences of which were to be an irreparable catastrophe.

Free to do as he liked, and master of an immense fortune, he had succeeded in obtaining admission to La Stilla's house, and had made her the offer of becoming Countess of Télek.

La Stilla had long known of the feelings with which she had inspired the young count. She had said to herself that he was a gentleman to whom any woman, even of the highest rank, would be happy to trust her life and happiness. And in the state of mind she then was, when Franz de Télek offered her his name, she received the offer with a sympathy she took no pains to hide. She felt herself loved in such a way that she consented to become the wife of Count Télek, and without regret abandon her dramatic career.

The news was then true; La Stilla would not appear again on any stage, as soon as the San Carlo season came to an end. In fact, her marriage, of which there had been some suspicions, was announced as certain.

This, as may be imagined, caused considerable excitement not only in the professional world, but in the fashionable world of Italy. After refusing to believe in the realization of this project, they had to admit it. Hatred and jealousy arose against the young count who was to take her away from her art, her success, the idolatry of the dilettanti, the greatest singer of her age. Even personal threats were directed against Franz de Télek—which threats in no way troubled him.

But if it was thus with the public, we can imagine what Rodolphe de Gortz felt at the thought of losing La Stilla, and that he would lose with her all that was life to him. There was a rumour that he was about to commit suicide. It was certain that from this day Orfanik was not seen in the streets of Naples. He never left Baron Rodolphe. Many times he was with him in the box which the baron occupied at every performance—and that he had never done before, being, like other learned men, absolutely refractory to the sensual charm of music.

The days, however, went by; the excitement did not subside, and it was at its height the last time La Stilla was to appear on the stage. It was in the superb character of Angelica in "Orlando," the masterpiece of Arconati, that she was to bid her farewell to the public.

That night San Carlo was but a tenth large enough to hold the people who crowded at its doors and for the most part remained outside. It was feared that there would be a manifestation against Count de Télek, if not while La Stilla was on the stage, at least when the curtain fell on the last act.

The Baron de Gortz had taken his place in his box, and this time Orfanik was again with him.

La Stilla appeared, more agitated than she had ever been. She recovered herself, however; she abandoned herself to her inspiration, and sang with such perfection, such ineffable talent, that the indescribable enthusiasm she excited among the audience rose almost to delirium.

During the performance the young count waited at the wing, impatient, nervous, feverish, cursing the length of the scenes, and angry at the delays provoked by the applause and recalls. Ah! how they hindered him from carrying off from this theatre her who was to be the Countess of Télek; the adored woman he would take far, far away, so far that she would belong but to him, to him alone.

At last came the final most dramatic scene, in which the heroine of Orlando dies. Never had the admirable music of Arconati appeared more impressive, never had La Stilla interpreted it with more impassioned emphasis. All her soul seemed to distil itself through her lips. And yet one would have said that this voice was about to break, for it was to be no longer heard.

At this moment the railing of the Baron de Gortz's box was lowered. Over it there appeared that strange head with the long grizzly hair and the eyes of flame. It showed itself, that ecstatic face, frightful in its pallor, and from the wing Franz saw it in the light for the first time.

La Stilla was then revelling in the full power of that ravishing stretto of the final air. She had just repeated that phrase with the sublime sentiment,— *"Inamorata, mio cuore tremante Voglio morire."*

Suddenly she stopped. Baron de Gortz's face terrified her. An inexplicable terror paralyzed her. She put her hand to her mouth; it reddened with blood. She staggered; she fell—

The audience rose, trembling, bewildered, distracted. A cry escaped from Baron de Gortz's box.

Franz rushed on to the stage; he took La Stilla in his arms; he lifted her, he looked at her, he called her.

"Dead! dead!" he cried. "She is dead!"

Yes! La Stilla was dead. A blood-vessel had broken. Her song died with her last sigh.

The young count was taken back to his hotel in such a state that his reason was despaired of. He was unable to be present at La Stilla's funeral, which took place amid an immense crowd of the Neapolitan population.

It was at the cemetery of Campo Santo Nuovo that the singer was buried, and all that could be read on the marble was— Stilla.

The night of the funeral a man went to the Campo Santo Nuovo. There with haggard eyes, bowed head, and lips clenched as if they had been sealed by death, he looked for a long time at the spot where La Stilla lay; and he seemed to listen as if the voice of the great artiste was to be heard for the last time from her grave.

It was Rodolphe de Gortz.

That very night the Baron de Gortz, accompanied by Orfanik, left Naples, and no one knew what became of him. But the next morning a letter was received by the young count. The letter contained but these words:—

It is you who have killed her. Woe to you, Count de Télek!

Rodolphe de Gortz

CHAPTER X.

Such had been this lamentable history.

For a month Franz de Télek's life was in danger. He recognized nobody—not even his man Rotzko. In the height of his fever but one name escaped his lips, which were ready to part with their last breath: it was that of La Stilla.

The young count did not die. The skill of the doctors, the incessant care of Rotzko, together with his own youth and constitution, saved Franz de Télek. His reason emerged uninjured from this terrible struggle. But when memory returned to him, when he recalled the final tragic scene in "Orlando," in which the soul of the artiste had left her,—

"Stilla! my Stilla!" he cried, stretching out his hands as if he were applauding.

As soon as his master could leave his bed, Rotzko persuaded him to leave this accursed town, and allow himself to be carried home to the Castle of Krajowa. But before he left Naples the young count wished to go and pray over the grave of the dead, and bid her a last and eternal farewell.

Rotzko accompanied him to Campo Santo Nuovo. There Franz threw himself on the cruel ground—he would have torn it up with his finger-nails to bury himself by her side. Rotzko at last managed to get him away from the grave, where he had left all his life and all his happiness.

A few days afterwards Franz de Télek had returned to Krajowa, to his old family estate. Here he lived for four years in absolute retirement, never leaving the castle. Neither time nor distance could alleviate his grief. He would have forgotten, but it was impossible. The remembrance of La Stilla, vivid as on the first day was bound up with his life, and the wound would close only with death.

At the time our story begins the young count had left the castle for some weeks. What long and pressing arguments Rotzko had had to prevail on his master to abandon the solitude in which he was wasting away! Consolation might be impossible, but an attempt at distraction might at least be made.

A plan of a tour was then decided on, which consisted in first visiting the Transylvanian provinces. Later, Rotzko hoped that the young count would agree to resume the European journey which had been interrupted by the sad events at Naples.

Franz de Télek had set out for only a short exploration. He and Rotzko had crossed the Wallachian plains up to the imposing mass of the Carpathians; they had been among the Vulkan defiles, and after an ascent of Retyezat and an excursion across the valley of the Maros, they had come for a rest to the village of Werst, to the "King Mathias" inn.

We know the state of affairs when Franz de Télek arrived, and how he had been informed of the incomprehensible occurrences of which the castle had been the scene. We also know how he had ascertained that the castle belonged to Baron Rodolphe de Gortz.

The effect produced by this name was too apparent for Master Koltz and the other notables not to notice it. And Rotzko would have cheerfully sent to the devil this Master Koltz, who had so inopportunely uttered it, and his stupid stories. Why should some ill-chance have brought Franz de Télek to this very village of Werst, in the neighbourhood of the Castle of the Carpathians!

The young count had become silent. His look, wandering from one to the other, only too clearly indicated the deep trouble of his mind, which he was seeking in vain to calm.

Master Koltz and his friends understood that some mysterious tie must exist between the Count de Télek and the Baron de Gortz; but, inquisitive as they were, they maintained a seemly reserve, and did not seek to take an advantage. Later on they would see what they could do.

A few minutes afterwards everyone had left the "King Mathias," much perplexed at this extraordinary chain of adventures, which foreboded no good to the village.

And now that the young count knew to whom the Castle of the Carpathians belonged, would he keep his promise? If he went to Karlsburg, would he report the matter to the authorities and demand their intervention? That was what the biro, the schoolmaster, Doctor Patak, and others were asking. If he did not do so, Master Koltz had resolved to do so. The police being informed of what had occurred, they would visit the castle, they would see if it were haunted by spirits or inhabited by criminals, for the village could remain no longer under such a state of affairs.

This would, it is true, be quite useless in the opinion of most of the inhabitants. To attack the spirits! The swords of the gendarmes would be broken like glass, and their guns would miss fire each time.

Franz de Télek, left alone in the large room of the "King Mathias," abandoned himself to the recollections which the name of Baron de Gortz had so unhappily evoked.

After remaining in an armchair for an hour, as if he were quite exhausted, he rose, left the saloon, and went out to the end of the terrace and looked away in the distance.

On the Plesa ridge, bounded by the Orgall plateau, rose the Castle of the Carpathians.

There had lived that strange personage, the frequenter of San Carlo, the man who had inspired such insurmountable terror in the unfortunate La Stilla. But at present the castle was deserted, and Baron de Gortz had not returned to it since he had fled from Naples. None knew what had become of him, and it was possible he had put an end to his existence after the death of the great artiste.

Franz wandered in this way across the field of supposition, knowing not where to stop. On the other hand, the adventure of the forester Nic Deck to a certain extent troubled him, and he would have liked to have unraveled the mystery, if it were only to reassure the people of Werst.

Added to this, the young count had no doubt that it was a band of thieves who had taken refuge in the castle, and he had resolved to keep his promise, and put a stop to the manœuvres of these sham ghosts by giving information to the police at Karlsburg.

But before taking steps in the matter, Franz resolved to have the most circumstantial details of the affair. For this object the best thing to do was to apply to the young forester in person; and about three o'clock in the afternoon, before returning to the inn, he presented himself at the biro's house.

Master Koltz showed that he was much honoured to receive a gentleman like the Count de Télek, this descendant of a noble Roumanian race, to whom the village of Werst would be indebted for the recovery of its peace and prosperity, for then travellers would return to visit the country, and pay the customary tolls, without having to fear the malevolent spirits of the Castle of the Carpathians, etc., etc.

Franz de Télek thanked Master Koltz for his compliments, and asked to be allowed to see Nic Deck if there were no objection.

"None at all, count," replied the biro. "The gallant Nic is going on as well as possible, and will soon return to his work."

And turning to his daughter, who had just entered the room, he said,—

"Is that not true, Miriota?"

"May Heaven grant it so, my father!" replied Miriota in an agitated voice.

Franz was charmed by the girl's graceful greeting. And seeing she was still anxious regarding the state of her betrothed, he hastened to ask her for some explanation on the subject.

"From what I have heard," he said, "Nic Deck has not been seriously hurt."

"No, count," said Miriota, "and Heaven be praised for it."

"You have a physician at Werst?"

"Hum!" said Master Koltz in a tone that was not very flattering to the old quarantine man.

"We have Doctor Patak," replied Miriota.

"He who accompanied Nic Deck to the Castle of the Carpathians?"

"Yes."

"I should like to see your betrothed for his own sake, and obtain the most precise details of this adventure."

"He will be glad to give you them, even though it may fatigue him a little."

"Oh! I will not abuse the opportunity. and I will do nothing that can injure Nic Deck."

"I know that."

"When is your marriage to take place?"

"In a fortnight," said the biro.

"Then I shall have the pleasure of being present, if Master Koltz will give me an invitation—"

"Such an honour, count—"

"In a fortnight, then, it is understood; and I am sure that Nic Deck will be well again as soon as he can take a walk with his good-looking betrothed."

"God protect him!" replied the girl as she blushed.

And her charming face betrayed such apparent anxiety that Franz asked her the reason.

"Yes, may God protect him!" replied Miriota; "for in endeavouring to enter the castle in spite of the prohibition, Nic has defied the spirits. And who knows if they may not set themselves to injure him all his life—"

"Oh! as for that," replied Franz, "we will have it all put straight, I promise you."

"Nothing will happen to my poor Nic?"

"Nothing; and, thanks to the police, you will be able to visit the castle in a few days, and be quite as safe as in the street at Werst."

The young count, thinking it inopportune to discuss the question of the supernatural, asked Miriota to show him the way to the forester's room.

This the girl hastened to do, and then she left him alone with her betrothed.

Nic Deck had been informed of the arrival of the two travellers at the "King Mathias" inn. Seated in an old armchair as large as a sentry-box, he rose to receive his visitor. As he now suffered but little from the paralysis with which he had been momentarily struck, he was sufficiently well to reply to the count's questions.

"Nic Deck," said Franz, after a friendly shake of the hand, "I would first ask you if you really believe in the presence of evil spirits at the Castle of the Carpathians?"

"I am compelled to believe it," replied Nic Deck.

"And it was they who kept you from getting over the castle wall?"

"I have no doubt of it."

"And why, if you please?"

"Because if they were not spirits, what happened to me would be inexplicable."

"Will you have the goodness to tell me, without omitting anything, what really did happen?"

"Willingly."

Nic Deck told his story item by item. He could only confirm the facts which Franz had heard in his conversation with the guests at the "King Mathias"—facts on which, as we know, the young count put a purely natural interpretation.

In short, the occurrences of this night of adventure could be easily explained if human beings, criminal or otherwise, occupied the castle, and had the machinery capable of producing these phantasmal effects. As to Doctor Patak's peculiar assertion that he was chained to the ground by some force, it could only be supposed that he had been the sport of some illusion. What was most likely was that his limbs had failed him simply because he was mad with terror, and that Franz declared to the young forester.

"What!" said Nic Deck, "would it be at the moment he wanted to run that his legs would fail the coward? That is hardly likely, you must admit."

"Well," continued Franz, "let us admit that his legs were caught in some trap, probably hidden under the grass at the bottom of the ditch."

"When a trap closes," said the forester, "it hurts you cruelly, it tears your flesh, and Doctor Patak's legs have no trace of a wound."

"Your observation is correct, Nic Deck; but if it be true that the doctor could not get away, it must be that his legs were caught in some snare."

"Then I will ask you how this snare could open of itself to set the doctor at liberty?"

Franz was too much puzzled to reply.

"But, count, I leave to you all that concerns Doctor Patak. After all, I can only speak of what I know of myself."

"Yes, let us leave the doctor, and speak of what happened to you, Nic Deck."

"What happened to me was clear enough. There is no doubt I received a terrible shock, and that in a way that is unnatural."

"There is no appearance of a wound on your body?" asked Franz.

"None; and yet I was struck with terrible violence."

"Was it just when you put your hand on the ironwork of the drawbridge?"

"Yes; just as I touched it, I seemed as if I were paralyzed. Fortunately my hand which held the chain did not leave go, and I slipped down into the bottom of the ditch, where the doctor found me senseless."

Franz shook his head with the air of a man whom these explanations left incredulous.

"You see," continued Nic Deck, "what I have told you is no dream; and if for eight days I remained full length on the bed, without the use of arms or legs, it is not reasonable to say I must have imagined it all."

"I do not attempt to do that," said the count; "it is only too certain you received a brutal shock."

"Brutal and diabolic."

"No—and in that we differ, Nic Deck. You believe you were struck by some supernatural being, and I do not believe there are supernatural beings, either good or evil—"

"Will you then explain what happened to me?"

"I cannot do that yet, Nic Deck; but rest assured all will be explained, and in a most simple manner."

"May God grant it so!"

"Tell me," said Franz, "has this castle belonged all along to the Gortz family?"

"Yes; and it belongs to it now, although the last descendant of the family, Baron Rodolphe, disappeared and no one has heard of him since."

"When did he disappear?"

"About twenty years ago."

"Twenty years?"

"Yes. One day Baron Rodolphe left the castle, of which the last servant died a few months after his departure; and no one has seen him since."

"And since then no one has set foot in the castle?"

"No one."

"And what is thought about him in the neighbourhood?"

"It is supposed that Baron Rodolphe died abroad a short time after he disappeared."

"Then it is supposed wrong, Nic Deck. The baron is still alive—at least he was so five years ago."

"He is alive?"

"Yes, in Italy—at Naples."

"You have seen him?"

"I have seen him?"

"And during the five years?"

"I have heard nothing about him."

The young forester thought for a moment or so. An idea had occurred to him, an idea he hesitated to formulate. At length he made up his mind, and, raising his head and knitting his brow, he said,—

"It is not supposable that Baron de Gortz has returned to the country with the intention of shutting himself up in the castle?"

"No—It is not supposable, Nic Deck."

"What object would he have in hiding himself, in never letting anybody come near him?"

"None," replied Franz de Télek.

And yet this was the thought which had begun to take shape in the mind of the young count. Was it not possible that this personage, whose existence had always been so enigmatic, had taken refuge in the castle after he left Naples? There, thanks to superstitious beliefs skilfully acted upon, would it not be easy for him to live in isolation, to defend himself against every unwelcome search, it being understood that he knew the state of mind that prevailed in the surrounding country?

But yet Franz thought it useless to launch the Werstians on this hypothesis. It would have been necessary to have put them in possession of facts which were too personal to him. Besides, he would have convinced no body, and that he saw clearly enough when Nic Deck added,—

"If it is Baron Rodolphe who is in the castle, we shall have to believe that Baron Rodolphe is the Chort, for only the Chort could have treated me in that way."

Desirous of not returning over the same ground, Franz changed the course of the conversation. After employing every means to reassure the young forester as to the consequences of his attempt, he made him promise not to renew it. That was not his affair, it was the business of the authorities, and the Karlsburg police would know how to discover the mystery of the Castle of the Carpathians.

The young count then took leave of Nic Deck, recommending him to get well as quickly as possible, so as not to delay his marriage with the fair Miriota, at which he promised to be present.

Absorbed in his reflections, Franz returned to the "King Mathias" and did not go out again that day.

At six o'clock Jonas served his dinner in the large room, when by a praiseworthy feeling of reserve neither Master Koltz nor any of the villagers came to trouble his solitude.

About eight o'clock Rotzko said to the young count,—

"You have no further need of me master?"

"No, Rotzko."

"Then I will go and smoke my pipe on the terrace."

"Go, Rotzko, go."

Lounging in an armchair, Franz again began to think of all that had passed. He was at Naples during the last performance at the San Carlo Theatre. He saw the Baron de Gortz at the moment when, for the first time, this man appeared to him, his head out of the box, his look ardently fixed on the artiste as if he would fascinate her.

Then his thoughts recurred to the letter signed by this strange personage, which accused him, Franz de Télek, of having killed La Stilla.

Lost in his recollections, Franz felt sleep come over him little by little. But he was still in that transition state when one can perceive the least noise, when a surprising phenomenon took place.

It seemed that a voice sweet and modulated made itself heard in this room where Franz was alone, quite alone.

Without knowing whether he dreamt or not, Franz rose and listened.

Yes! It seemed as though a mouth came close to his ear, and invisible lips gave forth the expressive melody of Stefano inspired by these words,—

Nel giardino de' mille fiori
Andiamo, mio cuore...

This romance Franz knew. This romance of ineffable sweetness La Stilla had sung in the concert she had given at the San Carlo Theatre before her farewell performance.

Unconsciously Franz abandoned himself to the charm of hearing it once again.

Then the phrase ended, and the voice, gradually growing fainter, died away with the last vibrations of the air.

But Franz roused himself from his torpor. He straightened himself up abruptly. He held his breath to seize some distant echo of this voice which went to his heart.

All was silent within and without.

"Her voice!" he murmured. "Yes! it was really her voice—the voice I loved so much."

Then returning to himself he said,—

"I was asleep, and I dreamed."

CHAPTER XI.

The count awoke at dawn, his mind still troubled with the visions of the night.

In the morning he was to leave the village of Werst on the road to Kolosvar.

After visiting the manufacturing towns of Petroseny and Livadzel, Franz's intention was to stay an entire day at Karlsburg, before stopping some time in the capital of Transylvania. From there the railway would take him across the provinces of Central Hungary, where his journey would end.

Franz had left the inn, and, walking on the terrace with his field-glass at his eyes, he was examining with deep emotion the outlines of the castle, which the sun was showing up so clearly on the Orgall plateau.

And his reflections bore on this point:—When he reached Karlsburg, would he keep the promise he had made to the people of Werst? Would he inform the police of what had happened at the Castle of the Carpathians?

When the young count had undertaken to restore peace to the village, he had no doubt but that the castle was the refuge of some gang of criminals, or, at least of people of doubtful repute, who having some interest in not being sought after, had taken steps to prevent anyone approaching them.

But since the previous day Franz had been thinking the matter over. A change had come over his thoughts, and he now hesitated.

For five years the last descendant of the family of Gortz, Baron Rodolphe, had disappeared, and what had become of him no one knew. Doubtless rumour had said he was dead, a short time after his departure from Naples. But was that true? What proof had they of his death? Perhaps the Baron de Gortz was alive; and if he lived, why should he not have returned to the castle of his ancestors? Why should not Orfanik, his only familiar friend, have accompanied him, and why should not this strange physician be the author and manager of these phenomena which caused such terror in the country?

It will be admitted that this hypothesis appeared somewhat plausible; and if Baron Rodolphe de Gortz and Orfanik had taken refuge in the castle, it was natural that they would try and make it unapproachable, so as to live that life of isolation which was in accordance with their habits and characters.

If this were the case, what ought the count to do? Was it desirable that he should interfere in the private affairs of the Baron de Gortz? This he was asking himself, weighing the pros and cons of the question, when Rotzko came to rejoin him on the terrace.

When he had told him of what he had been thinking,—

"Master," replied Rotzko, "it is possible that this may be the Baron de Gortz who is giving himself over to every diabolic imagination. Well, if that is so, my advice is not to mix ourselves up with his affairs. The poltroons of Werst will get out of their difficulty in their own way that is their business, and we have no reason for troubling ourselves about bringing peace to this village."

"Quite so," said Franz; "and all things considered, I think you are right, my brave Rotzko."

"I think so," said Rotzko simply.

"As to Master Koltz and the others, they now know what to do to finish up with the pretended spirits at the castle."

"Undoubtedly. All they have to do is to tell the Karlsburg police."

"We will start after breakfast."

"All will be ready."

"But before we return down the valley of the Syl, we will go round towards Plesa."

"And why?"

"I wish to see this Castle of the Carpathians a little nearer, if possible."

"For what purpose?"

"Fancy, Rotzko; a mere fancy, which will not delay us half a day."

Rotzko was much annoyed at this decision, which he looked upon as useless. All it could do would be to recall the memory of the past, which he tried his best to avoid. This time he tried in vain, and he had to yield to his master's inflexible resolution.

Franz, as if he had become subject to some irresistible influence, felt himself drawn towards the castle. Without his being aware of it, this attraction might be due to the dream in which he had heard the voice of La Stilla murmur the plaintive melody of Stefano.

But had he been dreaming? Yes, that is what he was asking himself now that he remembered that in this same room of the "King Mathias" a voice had already made itself heard—that voice which Nic Deck had so imprudently defied. In the count's mental condition there was nothing surprising in his forming the plan of going to the castle, to the foot of its wall, without any thought of entering.

Franz de Télek had, of course, no intention of telling the inhabitants of Werst of his journey. These people would doubtless have joined Rotzko in dissuading him from approaching the castle, and he had ordered his man to be silent regarding it. When they saw him descending the village towards the valley of the Syl, everybody imagined they were on their way to Karlsburg. But from the terrace he had remarked that another road skirted the base of Retyezat up to the Vulkan. It would thus be possible to climb the ridge of Plesa towards the castle without passing again through the village, and consequently without being seen by Master Koltz or the others.

About noon, having settled without discussion the somewhat inflated bill which Jonas presented to the accompaniment of his best smile, Franz prepared to leave Werst.

Master Koltz, the fair Miriota, Magister Hermod, Doctor Patak, the shepherd Frik, and a number of the other inhabitants had come to bid him farewell.

The young forester had even left his room, and it was clear enough would soon be on his legs again—for which the doctor took all the honour to himself.

"I congratulate you, Nic Deck," said Franz to him, "both you and your betrothed."

"We are much obliged to you," said the girl, radiant with happiness.

"May your journey be fortunate," added the forester.

"Yes—may it be so!" replied Franz, though his forehead was a little clouded.

"Monsieur le Comte," said Master Koltz, "we beg that you will not forget the information you promised to give at Karlsburg."

"I will not forget it, Master Koltz," replied Franz; "but should I be delayed on my journey, you know the very simple means of disembarrassing yourselves of your troublesome neighbours, and the castle will soon inspire no fear among the brave people of Werst."

"That is easily said," murmured the magister.

"And easily done," replied Franz. "Before forty-eight hours, if you like, the police will have settled up with whoever is hiding in the castle."

"Except in the very probable case that they are spirits," said the shepherd Frik.

"Even then," said Franz, slightly shrugging his shoulders.

"Monsieur le Comte," said Doctor Patak, "if you had accompanied me and Nic Deck, you might not talk about them as you do!"

"I should be astonished if I did not," replied Franz, "even if, like you, I had been so strangely detained by the feet in the castle ditch."

"By the feet—yes, count, or rather by the boots! Unless you suppose that in my state of mind I dreamt—"

"I suppose nothing," said Franz, "and will not try to explain what appears inexplicable. But be assured that if the gendarmes come to visit the Castle of the Carpathians, their boots, which are accustomed to discipline, will not take root like yours."

And with that parting shot at the doctor the count received for the last time the respects of the innkeeper of the "King Mathias"—so honoured to have had the honour of the honourable Franz de Télek, etc. After a salute to Master Koltz, Nic Deck, his betrothed, and the inhabitants in the road, he made a sign to Rotzko, and both set out at a good pace down the road.

In less than an hour Franz and his man had reached the right bank of the river which flowed round the southern base of Retyezat.

Rotzko had made up his mind to make no observation to his master; it would have been useless to have done so. Accustomed to obey him in military style, if the young count met with some perilous adventure he would know how to get him out of it.

After two hours' walking Franz and Rotzko stopped for a short rest.

At this place the Wallachian Syl, which had been curving gently towards the right, approached the road by rather a sharp turn. On the other side was the Plesa and the Orgall plateau, at the distance of about a league. Franz then had to leave the Syl if he wished to cross the hill in the direction of the castle.

Evidently this roundabout way, chosen for the purpose of avoiding a return through Werst, must have doubled the distance which separated the castle from the village. Nevertheless it was still broad daylight when Franz and Rotzko reached the crest of the Orgall plateau. The young count would thus have time to see the castle from the outside. Then he could wait until evening before going back towards Werst, and it would be easy to follow the road without being seen. Franz's intention was to pass the night at Livadzel, a little town situated at the confluence of the Syls, and to resume the road to Karlsburg in the morning.

The halt lasted half an hour. Franz, deep in his remembrances, much agitated at the thought that Baron de Gortz had perhaps concealed his existence in this castle, said not a word.

And Rotzko had to make a great effort to keep from saying to him,—

"It is useless to go further, master! Turn your back on this cursed castle and let us be off."

They began to follow the thalweg of the valley; but first they had to cross a thicket in which there was no footpath. Patches of the ground had been deeply cut into, for in the rainy season the Syl frequently overflows, and flows in tumultuous torrents over the ground, which it converts into marsh. This caused some difficulty in the advance, and consequently some delay; and it took an hour to get back on the Vulkan road, which was reached about five o'clock.

The right flank of Plesa is not covered with the forest such as Nic Deck had to cut his way through with an axe; but its difficulties were of another kind. There were heaps of moraines, among which they could not venture without caution; sudden changes of level, deep excavations, great blocks dangerously unsettled on their bases and standing up like the seracs of Alpine regions, all the confusion of the piles of enormous stones which avalanches had precipitated from the summit of the mountain-in fact, a veritable chaos in all its horror.

To climb a slope like this took a good hour's hard work. It seemed indeed that the Castle of the Carpathians was sufficiently defended by the impracticability of its approaches. And perhaps Rotzko hoped that there would be obstacles it would be impossible to surmount, although there were none.

Beyond the zone of blocks and hollows, the outer crest of the Orgall plateau was eventually reached. From there the outline of the castle was clear enough in the midst of this mournful desert, from which for so many years fear had kept a way the natives of the district.

It should be noticed that Franz and Rotzko had approached the castle on its northern face; Nic Deck and Doctor Patak had attacked it on the east by taking the left of the Plesa and leaving the torrent of Nyad to the right. The two directions formed a somewhat wide angle, of which the apex was the central donjon. On the northern side it was impossible to obtain admittance, for there was neither gate nor drawbridge, and the wall, in following the irregularities of the plateau, ran to a considerable height.

But it mattered little that access was impossible on this side, for the young count had no intention of entering within the walls.

It was half-past seven when Franz de Télek and Rotzko stopped at the extreme end of the Organ plateau. Before them rose this barbaric pile of buildings spread out in the gloom, and of much the same colour as that of the Plesa rocks. To the left, the wall made a sudden bend, flanked by the bastion at the angle. There, on the platform above the crenellated parapet stood the beech whose twisted branches bore witness to the violent south-westerly breezes at this height.

The shepherd Frik was not deceived; the legend gave but three more years of life to the old castle of the Barons of Gortz.

Franz in silence looked at the mass or buildings dominated by the stumpy donjon in the centre. There, without doubt, under that confused mass, were still hidden vaulted chambers long and sonorous, long dædalian corridors, and redoubts concealed in the ground such as the old Magyar fortresses still possess. No dwelling could have been more fit for the last descendant of the family of Gortz to bury himself in oblivion, of which none knew the secret. And the more the young count thought, the more he clung to the idea that Rodolphe de Gortz had taken refuge in the isolation of his Castle of the Carpathians.

But there was nothing to show that the donjon was inhabited. No smoke rose from its chimneys, no sound came from its closed windows. Nothing—not even the cry of a bird—troubled the silence of the gloomy dwelling.

For some minutes Franz eagerly gazed at this ring of wall, which once was full of the tumult of festival and the clash of arms. But he said nothing, for his mind was laden with oppressive thoughts and his heart with remembrances.

Rotzko, who respected the young count's mournful silence, took care to keep away from him, and did not interrupt him by a single remark. But when the sun went down behind the shoulder of the Plesa, and the valley of the two Syls began to be bathed in shadow, he did not hesitate to approach him.

"Master," he said, "the evening has come. It will soon be eight o'clock."

Franz did not appear to hear.

"It is time to start," said Rotzko, "if we are to reach Livadzel before the inns close."

"Rotzko—in a minute—yes—in a minute I will go with you," said Franz.

"It will take us quite an hour, master, to return to the hill road, and as the night will then have fallen, we shall run no risk of being seen."

"A few minutes more," said Franz, "and we will go down towards the village."

The count had not moved from the spot he had stopped at when he reached the plateau.

"Do not forget, master," continued Rotzko, "that in the dark it will be difficult to pass among those rocks. We could hardly do it in broad daylight. You must excuse me if I insist—"

"Yes—we will go, Rotzko. I am with you."

And it seemed as though Franz was helplessly detained before the castle, perhaps by one of those secret presentiments which the heart cannot account for. Was he, then, chained to the ground like Doctor Patak said he had been in the ditch at the foot of the curtain? No; his feet were free from every fetter. He could move about on the plateau as he chose, and, if he wished, nothing could have prevented him from going round the walls, skirting the edge of the counterscarp.

Perhaps he would do so?

So thought Rotzko, who said for the last time,—

"Are you coming, master?"

"Yes, yes!" replied Franz. And he remained motionless.

The Orgall plateau was already in darkness. The shadow of the hills had spread over the buildings, whose outlines were all vague and misty. Soon nothing would be visible if no light shone from the windows of the donjon.

"Come, master, come!" said Rotzko. And Franz was about to follow him, when on the platform of the bastion, where stood the legendary beech, there appeared an indistinct shape.

Franz stopped, looking at the shape, whose outline gradually became clearer.

. It was a woman with her hair undone, her hands stretched out, enveloped in a long white robe.

But this costume, was it not that which La Stilla wore in that final scene in "Orlando" in which Franz de Télek had seen her for the last time?

Yes! And it was La Stilla; motionless, with her arms stretched out towards the young count, her penetrating gaze fixed on him.

"She!" he cried.

And rushing towards the ditch he would have rolled to the foot of the wall if Rotzko had not stopped him.

But the apparition suddenly faded, and La Stilla was hardly visible for a minute.

Little did it matter. A second would have sufficed for Franz to recognize her, and these words escaped him:

"She! and alive!"

CHAPTER XII

Was it possible? La Stilla, whom Franz de Télek thought never to see again, had just appeared on the platform of the bastion! He had not been the sport of an illusion, and Rotzko had seen her as he had done! It was indeed the great artiste in her costume of Angelica, such as she had worn in public at her last performance at San Carlo.

The terrible truth flashed across the young count. This adored woman, who was to have been the Countess of Télek, had been shut up for five years in this castle amid the Transylvanian mountains! She whom Franz had seen fall dead on the stage had survived! While he had been carried almost dying to the hotel, the Baron Rodolphe must have found her and carried her off to the Castle of the Carpathians; and it was an empty coffin that the whole population had followed to the Santo Campo Nuovo of Naples!

It all appeared incredible, inadmissible, contrary to probability; and Franz said so to himself over and over again. Yes! But one thing was indubitable: La Stilla must have been carried off by the Baron de Gortz, for she too was in the castle! She was alive, for she had just appeared above the wall! That was an absolute fact.

The young count endeavoured to collect his thoughts, which were centred on one single object: to rescue from Rodolphe de Gortz La Stilla, who for five years had been a prisoner in the Castle of the Carpathians.

"Rotzko," said Franz in a breathless voice. "listen to me. Understand me at least; it seems as though my brain were going,—

"My master—my dear master!"

"At all costs I must enter this castle this very night."

"No; to-morrow."

"This night, I tell you! She is there. She has seen me as I saw her. She is waiting for me—"

"Well, I will follow you."

"No. I will go alone."

"Alone?"

"Yes."

"But how can you get into the castle when Nic Deck was not able to?"

"I will go in, I tell you."

"The gate is shut."

"It will not be so for me. I will seek for and I will find a breach. I will get through it."

"You do not wish me to accompany you, master? You do not wish it?"

"No! We will separate; and it is by leaving me that you will serve me."

"Shall I wait for you here?"

"No, Rotzko."

"Where shall I go, then?"

"To Werst—or rather—no—not to Werst," replied Franz. "There would be no use in those people knowing. Go down to Vulkan and stay the night there. If you do not see me, leave Vulkan in the morning—that is to say—no—wait a few hours. Then go to Karlsburg. There go to the chief of the police. Tell him all that has happened. Then return with his men. If necessary, storm the castle. Deliver her! Ah! She—alive—in the power of Rodolphe de Gortz!"

And as the young count uttered these broken sentences Rotzko noticed that his excitement increased, and manifested itself in the disordered ideas of one who was no longer master of himself.

"Go, Rotzko!" he cried for the last time.

"You wish me to?"

"I do."

At this formal injunction Rotzko could but obey; particularly as Franz had begun to leave him, and the darkness hid him from view.

Rotzko remained a few moments where he was, unable to decide on going away. Then the idea occurred to him that the count's efforts would be in vain; that he would not be able to enter the castle, nor even to get through the outer wall; that he would be compelled to return to the village of Vulkan—perhaps next morning, perhaps that night. The two of them would then go to Karlsburg, and what neither of them could do alone would be done by the police. They would settle with this Baron de Gortz; they would rescue the unfortunate La Stilla; they would search this Castle of the Carpathians; they would not leave one stone upon another, if necessary, even if all the fiends imaginable united to defend it.

And Rotzko descended the slopes of the Orgall plateau, so as to return to the Vulkan road.

Following the edge of the counterscarp, Franz had already gone round the bastion which flanked it on the left.

A thousand thoughts crowded in his mind. There was now no doubt about the presence of the Baron de Gortz in the castle, for La Stilla was a prisoner therein. It could only be the baron. La Stilla alive! But how could Franz get to her? How could he get her out of the castle? He did not know, but it must be done—and it would be done. The obstacles which Nic Deck could not overcome he would overcome. It was not curiosity which had brought him among these ruins, it was love for the woman he had found alive, yes, alive! After believing her to be dead, he would rescue her from Rodolphe de Gortz!

Doubtless Franz had said to himself that he could only obtain admission to the interior by means of the south curtain, in which the gate opened opposite the drawbridge; and seeing that it was impossible for him to scale the high walls, he continued to skirt the crest of the Orgall plateau, as soon as he had turned the angle at the bastion.

In broad daylight there would not have been much difficulty in this. At night—the moon was not yet up—a night all the darker from the mists which thicken on the mountains, it was more dangerous. To the danger of a false step, to the danger of a fall to the bottom of the ditch, was added that of stumbling against the rocks, and perhaps causing them to fall over him.

Franz went on, however, keeping as near as possible to the zigzags of the counterscarp, feeling his way hand and foot, to make sure he was not going astray. Sustained by superhuman strength, he also felt himself guided by an extraordinary instinct that could not deceive him.

Beyond the bastion stretched the south wall, that with which the drawbridge established communication when it was not raised against the gate.

When the bastion was passed, obstacles appeared to multiply. Among the huge rocks which covered the plateau, to follow the counterscarp was impossible, and he had to leave it. Figure a man endeavouring to traverse a field of Carnac in which the dolmens and menhirs were on no plan whatever; and not a mark to guide him, not a ray of light in the dark night.

Franz kept on, here climbing over a rock which barred his way, there creeping among the rocks, his hands torn with the thistles and brushwood, his head skimmed by the pairs of ospreys disturbed in their resting-places and flying off, uttering their horrible scream.

Ah! why did not the chapel bell clang as it had clanged for Nic Deck and the doctor? Why did not the intense light which had enveloped them stream up from between the battlements of the donjon? He would have headed towards the sound, he would have made towards the light, as the sailor towards the siren's whistle or the light house rays.

No! nothing but deep night bordered his view a few yards away.

This lasted for nearly an hour. When the ground began to slope to the left, Franz felt he was going wrong. Perhaps he had gone lower than the gate? Perhaps he was beyond the drawbridge?

He stopped, stamping his foot and wringing his hand. Which way should he go? Ah! how angry he was when he thought he would have to wait for the daylight! But then he would be seen by the people in the castle, he could not take them by surprise. Rodolphe de Gortz would be on his guard.

It was in the night-time that he must get into the enclosure, and Franz could not find his way in this darkness!

A cry escaped him—a cry of despair:

"Stilla!" he cried, "my Stilla!"

Did he think that the prisoner could hear him, that she could reply to him?

And yet a score of times he shouted the name, and the echoes of Plesa repeated it.

Suddenly Franz's eyes were on the alert. A ray of light pierced the darkness—a dazzling ray, and its source was at a considerable elevation.

"There is the castle—there!" he said, and from its position the light could only come from the central donjon.

In his mental excitement Franz did not hesitate to believe that it was La Stilla who showed him this light. There could be no doubt she had recognized him at the moment he had perceived her through the battlements of the bastion. And now she it was who had given the signal and showed him the road to follow to reach the gate.

Franz went towards the light, which increased with every step he took. As he had gone too far to the left on the plateau, he had to go back about twenty yards to the right, and after a few trials he regained the edge of the counterscarp.

The light shone in his face, and its height showed that it came from one of the windows of the donjon.

Franz was about to find himself faced by the last obstacles—insurmountable, perhaps.

In fact, if the gate were shut, the drawbridge raised, he would have to go down to the foot of the wall, and what would he do then, where it was fifty feet high in front of him?

Franz went on towards the place where the drawbridge would rest if the gate were open.

The drawbridge was down.

Without even stopping to think, Franz rushed on to the bridge and laid his hand on the gate.

The gate opened.

Franz rushed under the dark arch. But before he had taken a dozen steps the drawbridge was raised with a clatter against the gate.

Count Franz de Télek was a prisoner in the Castle of the Carpathians.

CHAPTER XIII.

The country people and travellers who passed backwards or forwards over the Vulkan hill knew only the Castle of the Carpathians from its exterior aspect. At the respectful distance at which fear kept the bravest of Werst and its environs, it presented to the eye but an enormous mass of rocks which they might take to be ruins.

But within the enclosure was the castle as dilapidated as they supposed? No; and within the shelter of its solid walls and buildings, the old feudal fortress could have accommodated quite a garrison.

Vast vaulted halls, deep excavations, innumerable corridors, courts of which the stonework was hidden beneath the lofty fence of herbage, subterranean redoubts to which the light of day never penetrated, narrow staircases contrived in the thickness of the walls, casemates lighted by narrow loopholes in the external wall, a central donjon with three floors of apartments sufficiently habitable, crowned by a crenellated platform; and among the other buildings of the enclosure, interminable corridors capriciously entangled, mounting to the platform of the bastions, diving to the depths of the lower structure, with a few cisterns in which the rain-water was caught, the overflow feeding the torrent of the Nyad, and then long tunnels, not stopped up as was believed, but giving access to the Vulkan road—such was the state of the Castle of the Carpathians, the geometrical plan of which was as complicated as that of the labyrinths of Porsena, of Lemnos, or of Crete.

As Theseus was led on by his love for the daughter of Minos, so was it the power of love, more intense and more irresistible, which had led the count within the intricacies of the castle. Would he find an Ariadne's thread to guide him, as the Greek hero had done?

Franz had had but one thought—to get within the enclosure, and he had got there. But one thing might have struck him, and that was that the drawbridge, which had always been raised, seemed to have been expressly lowered to admit him. Perhaps he might have been uneasy when the gate shut suddenly behind him? But he gave no thought to these things. He was at last in the castle where Rodolphe de Gortz was keeping La Stilla, and he would sacrifice his life to reach her.

The gallery into which Franz had advanced was wide, lofty, and with a vaulted roof, and it was quite dark, and its pavement was broken up, so that it had to be trodden carefully.

Franz took to the left wall, and kept to it, feeling his way along the facing, the efflorescent surface of which rubbed off on his hands. He heard no sound except that of his steps, which echoed in the distance. A draught of warm air with an ancient, frowsy smell swept gently past him, as if there were an opening at the other end of the gallery.

After passing a stone pillar which served as a buttress in the last angle to the left, Franz found himself in a much narrower corridor. He had only to open his arms to touch the walls.

He went on in this way, his body bent forward, feeling with hands and feet, and endeavouring to discover if the passage were a straight one.

Two hundred yards after passing the buttress Franz felt the wall curving off to the left, to take the exactly opposite direction fifty paces farther on. Did it return to the outer wall, or did it lead to the foot of the donjon?

Franz endeavoured to quicken his advance, but every moment he was hindered by a rise in the ground, against which he stumbled, or by some sharp angle which changed his direction. From time to time he would reach some opening in the wall leading off to lateral ramifications. But all was dark, unfathomable, and it was in vain he sought to make out where he was in this maze in a molehill.

He had to retrace his steps several times on ascertaining that he had gone where there was no thoroughfare. One thing he had to fear was that some badly-fastened trap door would give way under his feet and drop him into some underground cell from which he could not escape. And so whenever he touched a piece that sounded hollow he took care to cling to the walls, though he went forward with an ardour that hardly left him time for reflection.

At the same time, as he had neither gone upwards nor downwards, the floor was clearly on the level of the inner courts arranged among the different buildings within the enclosure, and it was possible that the passages ended in the central donjon, perhaps at the foot of the stair case.

Certainly there ought to exist a more direct means of communication between the gate and the central buildings. When the Gertz family had lived there it had not been necessary to enter these interminable passages. A second gate, which faced the gate opposite the first gallery, opened on to the place of arms, in the centre of which rose the keep; but it had been stopped up, and Franz had not been able to see where it had been.

For an hour the young count continued his advance at a venture, listening if he could hear any distant sound, and not daring to shout for La Stilla lest the echoes should carry it to the upper floors of the donjon. He was in no way discouraged, and would go on until strength failed him, or some impassable obstacle compelled him to stop.

But although he took no notice of it, Franz was already nearly exhausted. Since he left Werst he had eaten nothing. He suffered from hunger and thirst. His step was not sure, his legs were failing him. In this warm, humid air his respiration had become irregular, and his heart beat violently.

It was nearly nine o'clock when Franz, putting out his left foot, found no ground to tread upon.

He stooped down and felt there was a step, and then another below it.

It was a staircase.

Did these stairs go down to the foundations of the castle, with no way of exit.?

Franz did not hesitate to go down them, and he counted the steps, which went off obliquely from the passage.

Seventy-seven steps were thus descended to the level of a second passage which led to many gloomy windings.

Franz went along these for half an hour, and, tired out, had just stopped when a luminous point appeared several hundred feet in advance.

Whence came this light? Was it merely a natural phenomenon, the hydrogen of some will-o'the-wisp that had lighted itself at this depth? Was it a lantern carried by one of the inhabitants of the castle?

"Can it be La Stilla?" murmured Franz. And the thought occurred to him that a light had already appeared as if to show him the way into the castle when he was wandering among the rocks on the Orgall plateau. If it had been La Stilla who had shown this light at one of the windows of the donjon, was it not La Stilla who was now trying to guide him amid the sinuosities of these subterranean passages?

Hardly master of himself, Franz bent down and looked ahead without moving. It was more a diffused effulgence than a luminous point that seemed to fill a sort of vault at the end of the passage.

Franz crawled towards it, for his limbs could scarcely support him, and passing through a narrow entrance he fell on the threshold of a crypt.

This crypt was in a good state of preservation, about twelve feet high, and circular in shape. The arches of the vault sprang from the capitals of eight dwarf columns, and met in a hanging boss, in the centre of which was a glass vase filled with a yellowish light.

Facing the entrance, between two of the columns, was another door which was closed, and the large rounded bolts showed where the outer ironwork of the hinges was fastened.

Franz dragged himself up to this second door and tried to move it.

His efforts were in vain.

Some old furniture was in the crypt; there was a bed, or rather a bench, in old heart-of-oak, on which were a few bedclothes; there was a stool with twisted feet; there was a table fixed to the wall with iron tenons. On the table were a large jug full of water, a dish with a piece of cold venison, a thick piece of bread like a sea-biscuit. In a corner murmured a fountain fed by a narrow stream, the overflow of which passed away at the base of one of the columns.

Did not these arrangements show that some guest was expected in this crypt, or rather a prisoner in this prison? Was this prisoner Franz? and had he been lured by a stratagem into the interior of the castle?

In the trouble of his thoughts Franz had no suspicion of this. Exhausted by want and fatigue, he dashed at the food on the table, quenched his thirst with the contents of the jug, and then fell on the rough bed, where a sleep of a few minutes might recruit his strength.

But when he tried to collect his thoughts it seemed as though they escaped like the water he might try to hold in his hand.

Would he then have to wait for daylight to recommence his search? Had his will so far forsaken him that he was no longer master of his acts?

"No," said he, "I will not wait! To the donjon! I must reach the donjon to-night."

Suddenly the light in the vase went out, and the crypt was plunged in complete darkness.

Franz would have risen. He could not do so, and his thoughts went to sleep, or rather stopped suddenly, like the hand of a clock when the spring breaks. It was a strange sleep, or rather an overpowering torpor, an absolute annihilation of being, which did not proceed from the soothing of the mind.

How long the sleep lasted Franz did not know. His watch had run down and did not show the time. But the crypt was again bathed in artificial light.

Franz jumped off the bed, and stepped towards the first door, which was open all the time, then towards the second, which was still closed.

He began to reflect, and found he could not do so without difficulty.

If his body had recovered from the fatigues of the night before, he felt his head empty and heavy,

"How long have I slept?" he asked. "Is it night or is it day?"

Within the crypt nothing had changed, except that the light had been renewed, the food replaced, and the jug filled with clear water.

Some one, then, must have been there while Franz was deep in this overpowering slumber? It was known that he was in the depths of the castle! He was in the power of Baron Rodolphe de Gortz! Was he doomed to have no further communication with his fellow-men?

That was not possible, and, besides, he would escape, for he could do so; he would re-traverse the gallery that led to the gate, he would leave the castle.

Leave? He then remembered that the gate was closed behind him.

Well! He would try to reach the outer wall, and by one of the embrasures he would try to slip down into the ditch. Cost what it might, in an hour he would have escaped from the castle.

But La Stilla? Would he give up reaching her?

Would he go away without rescuing her from Rodolphe de Gortz?

Yes! And what he could not do single-handed he would do with the help of the police, which Rotzko would bring from Karlsburg to the village of Werst. They would rush to the assault of the old stronghold, they would search the castle from top to bottom.

Having come to this determination, he decided to put it into execution without losing an instant.

Franz rose, and was walking towards the passage by which he had come, when he heard a noise behind the other door.

It was certainly the sound of footsteps approaching very slowly.

Franz put his ear against the door and, holding his breath, he listened intently.

The steps seemed to come at regular intervals, as if they were going upstairs. No doubt there was a second staircase which connected the crypt with the interior courts.

In readiness for whatever might happen, Franz drew from the sheath his hunting-knife, which he wore at his belt, and gripped it firmly.

If it were to be one of the Baron de Gortz's servants who entered, he would throw himself on him, take away the keys, and make it impossible for him to follow him. And then Franz would rush along this new road and try to reach the donjon.

If it were the Baron de Gortz—and he would recognize him, although he had only seen him once, at the moment La Stilla fell on the stage of San Carlo—he would attack him without mercy.

However, the footsteps stopped on the landing which formed the outer threshold.

Franz did not move, but waited until the door was opened.

It did not open, but a voice of infinite sweetness was heard by the young count.

It was the voice of La Stilla—yes!—her voice a little weakened, her voice which had lost nothing of its inflections, of its inexpressible charm, or its caressing modulations, that admirable instrument of its marvellous art, which seemed to have died with the artiste.

And La Stilla repeated the plaintive melody which he had heard in his dream when he slept in the saloon of the inn at Werst:-

Nel giardino de' mille fiori
Andiamo, mio cuore...

The song entered into Franz to the depths of his soul. He breathed it, he drank it like a divine liquor, while La Stilla seemed to invite him to follow her, repeating,—

Andiamo, mio cuore...andiamo.

But why did not the door open to let him through? Could he not reach her, clasp her in his arms, take her with him out of the castle?

"Stilla—my Stilla!" he shouted, and he threw himself against the door, which stood firm against his efforts.

Already the song seemed to grow fainter, the footsteps were heard going away.

Franz knelt down, trying to shake the planks, tearing his hands with the ironwork, calling all the time to La Stilla, whose voice had died away in the distance.

It was then that a terrible thought flashed through his mind.

"Mad!" he exclaimed. "She is mad, for she did not recognize me and did not reply to me. For five years she has been shut up in this castle, in the power of this man—my poor Stilla—her reason has left her!"

Then he rose, his eyes haggard, his head as if on fire.

"I also—I feel that I am going mad!" he repeated; "I am going mad—mad like her!"

He strode backwards and forwards across the crypt like a wild beast in its cage.

"No!" he repeated. "No! I must not go mad. I must get out of this castle. I will go!"

And he went towards the first door. It had just shut silently.

Franz had not noticed it while he was listening to the voice of La Stilla.

He had been imprisoned within the enclosure, and now he was a prisoner within the crypt.

CHAPTER XIV.

Franz was thoroughly astounded. As he had feared, the faculty of thinking, of comprehending matters, the intelligence necessary for him to reason on them, was gradually leaving him. The only feeling that remained was the remembrance of La Stilla, the impression of the song he had just heard, and which the echoes of this gloomy crypt no longer repeated.

Had he been the sport of an illusion? No, a thousand times no! It was indeed La Stilla he had just heard, it was indeed her he had seen on the castle bastion.

Then the thought returned to him, the thought that she was deprived of reason, and this horrible blow struck him as if he were about to go out of his mind a second time.

"Mad!" he repeated. "Yes! Mad—for she did not recognize my voice—mad—mad!"

And that seemed to be only too likely. Ah! if he could only rescue her from this place, take her to his Castle of Krajowa, devote himself entirely to her, his care and love would soon restore her to sanity.

So said Franz, a prey to a terrible delirium, and many hours went by before he was himself again.

Then he tried to reason coolly, to collect himself amid the chaos of his thoughts.

"I must get away from here," he said. "How? As soon as they reopen that door! Yes! During my sleep they come and renew this food, I will wait—I will pretend to sleep."

A suspicion occurred to him. The water in the jug must contain some soporific substance. If he had been plunged in this heavy sleep, in this complete unconsciousness, the duration of which he did not know, it was because he had drunk this water. Well, he would drink no more of it. He would not even touch the food on the table. Somebody would come soon and then—

Then! What did he know of it? At this moment was the sun mounting towards the zenith or sinking on the horizon? Was it day or night?

Then Franz listened for the sound of footsteps at either door. But no sound reached him. He crept along the walls of the crypt, his head burning, his eyes glaring, his ears throbbing, his breath panting amid this heavy atmosphere, which was only just renewed through the chink around the doors.

Suddenly near the angle of one of the columns on the right he felt a fresher breath than usual reach his lips.

Was there an opening here through which air came in from the outside?

Yes; there was a passage he had not noticed in the shade of the column.

To glide between the walls, to make for an indistinct clearness which seemed to come from above, was what Franz did in an instant.

There was a small court five or six yards across, with the walls a hundred feet high. It seemed to be a well which served as an outer court for this subterranean cell, and gave it a little air and light.

Franz could see it was still day. At the top of the well was a small angle of light which just shone on the upper margin.

The sun had accomplished at least half its diurnal course, for this luminous angle was slowly decreasing.

It must be about five o'clock in the afternoon. Consequently Franz must have slept for at least forty hours, and he had no doubt this must have been due to a soporific draught. As he and Rotzko had left Werst on the 11th of June, this must be the 13th which was about to finish in a few hours.

So humid was the air at the bottom of this court, that Franz breathed it deeply and felt all the better for it. But if he had hoped that an escape was possible up this long stone tube he was soon undeceived. To try and climb that smooth, lofty wall, was impracticable.

Franz returned to the interior of the crypt. As he could only get out through one of the doorways, he came to see what state they were in.

The first door-that by which he had come—was very solid and very thick, and was kept in its place on the other side by bolts working into iron staples; it was, therefore, useless to try and force it.

The second door—behind which he had heard La Stilla's voice—did not seem to be so well preserved. The boards were rotten in places, and it might be possible to clear a way through them.

"Yes—this is the way!" said Franz, who had recovered his coolness; "this is the way!"

But he had no time to lose, as it was probable some one would enter the crypt as soon as he was supposed to be asleep under the influence of the soporific draught.

The work went on more quickly than he had expected.

The moisture had eaten into the wood around the metal clasp which held the bolts against the embrasure. With his knife Franz managed to get the round part off, working noiselessly, and stopping now and then to listen and make sure that nothing was moving on the other side.

Three hours afterwards the bolts were free and the door opened with a scroop on its hinges.

Franz then returned to the little court so as to breathe a less stifling air.

At this moment the sun no longer shone across the opening of the well, and consequently must have sunk behind Retyezar. The court was in complete darkness. A few stars gleamed above, as if they were seen through the tube of a long telescope. A few small clouds drifted along in the intermittent breath of the night breeze. A peculiar haze in the atmosphere showed that the moon must have risen above the eastern mountains. It was evidently about nine o'clock at night.

Franz went back to the crypt, where he ate some of the food and quenched his thirst from the spring, after throwing away the liquid in the jug. Then, with his knife at his belt, he went out by the door, which he shut behind him.

And now would he meet the unfortunate La Stilla wandering in these subterranean galleries? At the thought his heart beat almost ready to burst.

As soon as he had made a few steps he stumbled. As he had thought, there was a flight of stairs, of which he counted the steps; sixty only instead of the seventy-seven he had come down to the threshold of the crypt. Consequently he was about eight feet below the level of the ground.

Having nothing better to do than to follow the dark corridor, the sides of which he could touch with his out stretched hands, he hurried on in that direction.

And he went on for half an hour without being stopped by door or railing. But the large number of turns had prevented him from knowing in what direction he was going with regard to the wall which faced the Orgall plateau.

After halting a few minutes to get his breath, Franz continued his advance, and it seemed as though the corridor were to be interminable, when an obstacle stopped him.

This was a wall of bricks.

Tapping it at different heights, he could find no sign of an opening.

This was the only way out from the corridor.

Franz could not help exclaiming. All his hopes were shattered against this obstacle. His knees bent, his legs gave way, and he fell at the foot of the wall.

But just on the ground the wall had a narrow crack in it, and the bricks, being rather loose, shook as he touched them.

"That is the way!" said Franz. "Yes! that is the way!"

And he began to pull out the bricks one by one, when there was a noise of something metallic on the other side.

Franz stopped.

The noise had not ceased, and at the same time a ray at light swept across the hole.

Franz looked through.

It was the old chapel that he saw. To what a lament able state of dilapidation time and neglect had reduced it!—the roof half fallen in, a few only of the ribs perfect on their swelling columns, two or three pointed arches threatening to fall, a window-frame with flamboyant mullions thrust out of place; here and there a dusty tomb beneath which slept some ancestor of the family of Gortz, and at the end a fragment of an altar with the reredos still showing traces of sculpture; then the remains of the roof still over the apse which had been spared by the storms, and then over the ridge above the entrance the shaking belfry from which hung a rope to the ground—the rope of the bell which occasionally rang to the terror of the people of Werst.

Into this chapel, deserted for so long, open to all the rigours of the Carpathian climate, a man had just entered, holding in his hand a lantern, the brilliant light of which shone full on his face.

Franz instantly recognized him. It was Orfanik, that eccentric individual whom the baron had made his only companion during his sojourn in the large Italian towns, that oddity he had seen along the streets gesticulating and talking to himself, that incomprehensible scientist, that inventor ever in search of some chimera, and who doubt less put all his inventions at the service of Rodolphe de Gortz.

If Franz had retained any doubt as to the presence of the baron at the Castle of the Carpathians, even after the apparition of La Stilla, this doubt was changed to certainty when he saw Orfanik.

What was he going to do in this ruined chapel at this advanced hour of the night?

Franz tried to discover, and this is what he saw.

Orfanik, stooping over the ground, was lifting up a few iron cylinders to which he was attaching a line, which he unrolled from a reel placed in one of the corners of the chapel. And such was the attention he gave to his work, that he would not even have seen the young count if he had been able to get near him.

Ah! why was not the hole Franz had begun to enlarge sufficient to let him pass? He would have entered the chapel, he would have hurled himself on Orfanik, he would have compelled him to lead him to the donjon.

But perhaps it was as well that he could not do so, for if the attempt failed, the Baron de Gortz would have doubtless made him pay with his life for the secrets he had discovered.

A few minutes after the arrival of Orfanik another man entered the chapel.

It was Baron Rodolphe de Gortz. The never-to-be-forgotten physiognomy of this personage had not changed.

He did not even seem to have aged, with his pale, long face, which the lantern illuminated from top to bottom, his long grey hair thrown back behind his ears, and his look glittering from the depths of his black orbits.

Rodolphe de Gortz went near to examine the work on which Orfanik was engaged.

And this was the conversation exchanged between the men in short, sharp tones.

CHAPTER XV.

"Is the connection with the chapel finished, Orfanik?"

"I have just done it."

"Everything is ready in the casemates of the bastions?"

"Everything."

"The bastions and chapel are in direct connection with the donjon?"

"They are."

"And after the instrument has made the current, we shall have time to get away?"

"We shall."

"Have you made sure that the tunnel on to the Vulkan is clear?"

"It is."

They were silent for a few minutes while Orfanik took up his lantern and directed its light into the corners of the chapel.

"Ah! my old castle!" exclaimed the baron. "You will cost them dear who would storm your walls."

And Rodolphe de Gortz pronounced these words in a tone which made the count shudder.

"You have heard what they say at Werst?" the baron asked Orfanik.

"Fifty minutes ago I heard on the wire what they were talking about at the 'King Mathias.'"

"Is the attack to be to-night?"

"No, not until daybreak."

"When did this Rotzko return to Werst?"

"Two hours ago, with the police he brought from Karlsburg."

"Well! as the castle cannot defend itself," said the baron, "at least it can crush under its ruins this Franz de Télek and all his people with him."

Then, after a few moments he continued,—

"And this wire, Orfanik? Will they ever know that it put the castle in communication with the village of Werst?"

"I will destroy it, and they will know nothing about it."

And now the hour would seem to have come to explain certain phenomena which have occurred in the course of our story, the origin of which ought no longer to be concealed.

At this period—it must be remembered that these events happened in one of the closing years of the nineteenth century—the use of electricity, which has justly been called the soul of the universe, had been brought to its highest perfection. The illustrious Edison and his disciples had finished their work.

Among other electrical instruments, the telephone then worked with such wonderful precision that the sounds collected by the diaphragms could be freely heard without the aid of ear-trumpets. What was said, what was sung, what was even whispered, could be heard at any distance, and two persons separated by thousands of leagues could converse as easily as if they were side by side.

For some years Orfanik, the baron's inseparable companion, had been in all that concerns the practical application of electricity an inventor of the first order. But, as we know, his admirable discoveries had not been welcomed as they deserved. The learned world had taken him for a madman, whereas he was a man of genius; and hence the inappeasable hatred which the despised inventor bore to his fellow-men.

It was under these circumstances that Baron de Gortz had met Orfanik, who was then in the depths of misery. He encouraged him in his work, he helped him with money, and finally he engaged him to be his companion on condition that he alone should profit by his inventions.

In fact, these two eccentric personages were made to understand one another, and since their meeting they had never separated, not even when the Baron de Gortz was following La Stilla from town to town in Italy.

While the melomaniac was intoxicating himself with the singing of the incomparable artiste, Orfanik was busy in completing the discoveries made by electricians during these later years, perfecting their adaptations and obtaining the most extraordinary results from them.

After the events which terminated the dramatic career of La Stilla, the baron had disappeared without anyone knowing what had become of him. When he left Naples it was in the Castle of the Carpathians that he had taken refuge, accompanied by Orfanik, who had no hesitation in shutting himself up with him.

When he resolved to bury his existence in this old castle, the baron's intention was that no inhabitant of the district should suspect his return, and no one try to visit him. We need not say that Orfanik and he had the means of providing liberally for their daily wants; in fact, a secret communication existed with the road over the Vulkan, and by this road an old servant of the baron's, whom nobody knew, brought in all that was necessary for the existence of Baron Rodolphe and his companion.

In reality what remained of the castle—and particularly the central donjon—was less dilapidated than was believed, and even more habitable than its inmates required. Orfanik, provided with all he wanted for his experiments, busied himself with immense researches in physics and chemistry, and of these he proposed to avail himself in his attempt to keep off unwelcome visitors.

The Baron de Gortz received the propositions with eagerness, and Orfanik built special machinery for spreading terror in the country by producing phenomena which could only be ascribed to diabolic agencies.

But in the first place it was necessary for the Baron de Gortz to be kept informed of what was passing in the nearest village. Was there any means of hearing what its people were talking about without their suspecting anything? Yes, if a telephone communication could be established between the castle and the large saloon of the "King Mathias," where the notables of Werst were accustomed to meet every evening.

Orfanik managed this very skilfully and very secretly, and in the most simple manner. A copper wire covered with an insulating sheath had one end fastened on the first floor of the donjon and was then laid under the waters of the Nyad up to the village of Werst. This part of the work being accomplished, Orfanik, going himself out as a tourist, came to spend a night at the "King Mathias," and there connect the wire with the inn saloon. It was easy for him to bring up the end from the bed of the torrent to the height of the back window, which was never opened. He then fixed a telephonic instrument, which was hidden by the thick foliage, and with that connected the cable. As the instrument was ingeniously adapted to emit as well as to receive sound, Baron de Gortz could hear all that was said at the "King Mathias," and make himself heard whenever he chose.

During the first years the tranquillity of the castle was not troubled. The evil reputation it enjoyed was enough to keep the people of Werst away from it. But one day, that on which our story began, the purchase of the telescope led to the smoke being noticed escaping from the donjon chimney. From that moment interest was reawakened, and we know what happened.

It was then that the telephonic communication proved useful, for the baron and Orfanik could keep themselves posted up in what was passing in the village. It was by the wire that they knew that Nic Deck had undertaken to visit the castle, and by the wire the threatening voice entered the room to endeavour to keep him away. When the young forester persisted in his determination in spite of the menace, the baron resolved to give him such a lesson that he would have no desire to try it again. That night, Orfanik's machinery, which was always in working order, produced a series of purely physical phenomena intended to carry terror throughout the district; the bell was rung in the old chapel, intense flames were shot forth mingled with sea-salt, giving a spectral appearance to everything; powerful sirens were worked from which the compressed air escaped in terrible groans; diagram outlines of monsters were projected on to the clouds by means of huge reflectors; iron plates were laid about the ditch in communication with electric batteries, and one of these plates caught the doctor by his iron-shod boots, while another had given the forester a shock at the moment he laid his hand on the drawbridge.

And so the baron thought that after the apparition of these prodigies, after the attempt of Nic Deck which had ended so badly, terror would reach its height in the district, and that neither for gold nor silver would anyone approach even within two good miles of this Castle of the Carpathians, evidently haunted by supernatural beings.

Rodolphe de Gortz thought himself safe from all unwelcome curiosity when Franz de Télek arrived in the village of Werst.

All that passed between him and Jonas and Master Koltz and the others was immediately known to him along the wire in the Nyad. The baron's hatred of the young count was rekindled by the memory of the events which had occurred at Naples. And not only was Franz de Télek in the village, a few miles from the castle, but there before the notables he was deriding their absurd superstitions, and demolishing that fantastic reputation which protected the Castle of the Carpathians; and he was even undertaking to warn the Karlsburg authorities, so that the police might come and scatter the legends to the winds!

And so the Baron de Gortz resolved to allure Franz de Télek to the castle, and we know by what means he had succeeded. The voice of La Stilla, sent into the inn saloon by means of the telephone, had led the young Count to turn aside from his road to visit the castle; the apparition of the singer on the platform of the bastion hall given him an irresistible desire to enter; a light shown at one of the windows of the donjon had guided him to the gate, which was opened to let him in. In this crypt, lighted electrically, in which he had again heard that wonderful voice, and where food was brought him while he was in a lethargic sleep; in that crypt in the depths of the castle, the door of which was closed on him, Franz de Télek was in the power of the Baron de Gortz, and the Baron de Gortz intended he should never get out of it.

Such were the results obtained by this mysterious collaboration between Rodolphe de Gortz and his accomplice Orfanik. But to his extreme disgust. the barren knew that the alarm had been given by Rotzko, who not having followed his master into the castle, had warned the authorities at Karlsburg. A detachment of police had arrived at the village of Werst, and the Baron de Gortz would have a strong force to contend with. How could he and Orfanik defend themselves against a numerous party? The means employed against Nic Deck and Doctor Patak would not be enough, for the police do not believe in diabolic intervention. And so they had resolved to destroy the castle completely, and were only waiting for the moment to act. An electric current had been prepared for firing the charges of dynamite which had been buried in the donjon, the bastions, and the old chapel, and the arrangement would allow of the baron and his accomplice having time to escape by the tunnel on to the Vulkan road. After the explosion, of which the count and a number of those who had scaled the castle wall would be the victims, the two would get so far away that no trace of them would be discoverable.

What he had just heard had given Franz the explanation of many things that had happened. He now knew that telephonic communication existed between the Castle of the Carpathians and the village of Werst. He also knew that the castle was about to be destroyed in an explosion which would cost him his life and be fatal to the police brought by Rotzko. He knew that the Baron de Gortz and Orfanik would have time to get away, dragging with them the unconscious La Stilla.

Ah! why could not Franz rush into the chapel and throw himself on these men? He would have knocked them down, he would have stopped their injuring anyone, he would have prevented the catastrophe.

But what was impossible at the moment might not be so after the baron's departure. When the two had left the chapel Franz would throw himself on their track, pursue them to the castle, and with God's help would settle with them.

The baron and Orfanik were already in the apse. Franz had not lost sight of them. Which way were they going out? Was there a door opening on to the enclosure? or was there some corridor connecting the chapel with the donjon? for it seemed as though all the castle buildings were in communication with each other. It mattered little if the count did not meet with an obstacle he could not surmount.

At this moment a few words were interchanged between Baron de Gortz and Orfanik:—

"There is nothing more to do here?"

"Nothing."

"Then we can leave each other."

"You still intend that I should leave you alone in the castle?"

"Yes, Orfanik; and you get off at once by the tunnel on to the Vulkan road."

"But you?"

"I shall not leave the castle until the last moment."

"It is understood that I am to wait for you at Bistritz?"

"At Bistritz."

"Remain here, Baron Rodolphe, and remain alone, if that is your wish."

"Yes—for I wish to hear her—to hear her once again during this last night I shall pass in the Castle of the Carpathians."

A few moments afterwards the Baron de Gortz and Orfanik had left the chapel.

Although La Stilla's name had not been mentioned in this conversation, Franz understood; it was of her that Rodolphe de Gortz had just spoken.

CHAPTER XVI.

The catastrophe was imminent. Franz could only prevent it by rendering the baron incapable of executing his plan.

It was then eleven o'clock at night. With no further fear of being discovered, Franz resumed his work. The bricks were easily taken out of the wall, but its thickness was such that half an hour elapsed before the opening was large enough to admit him through.

As soon as he set foot in this chapel, open to all the winds that blew, he felt himself refreshed by the night air. Through the gaps in the roof and window-frames the sky could be seen, with the light clouds driving before the breeze. Here and there were a few stars, which were growing pale in the light of the moon now rising on the horizon.

Franz's object was to find the door which opened at the end of the chapel, by which the Baron de Gortz and Orfanik had gone out; and, crossing the nave obliquely, he advanced towards the apse.

This was in the darkness where none of the moonlight penetrated, and his foot stumbled against the ruins of the tombs and the fragments fallen from the roof.

At last, at the very end of the apse, behind the reredos, in a dark corner Franz felt a mouldy door yield before his hand.

This door opened on a gallery which apparently traversed the outer wall.

By it the baron and Orfanik had entered the chapel, and by it they had just departed.

As soon as Franz was in the gallery, he again found himself in complete darkness. After winding about a good deal without either a rise or a fall, he was certain that he was now on a level with the interior courts.

Half an hour later the darkness did not seem to be so deep; a kind of half-light glided through several lateral openings in the gallery.

Franz was able to walk faster, and reached a large casemate contrived under the platform of the bastion which flanked the left angle of the outer wall.

This casemate was pierced with narrow loopholes, through which streamed the rays of the moon.

In the opposite wall was an open door.

Franz's first care was to place himself at one of the loopholes so as to breathe the fresh night breeze for a few seconds.

But just as he was moving away he thought he saw two or three shadowy shapes moving at the lower end of the Orgall plateau, which was now full in the moonlight up to the sombre masses of the pine-forest

Franz looked again.

A few men were moving about on the plateau just in front of the trees—doubtless the Karlsburg police brought by Rotzko. Had they, then, decided to attack that night in the hope of surprising the occupants of the castle, or were they waiting for daybreak?

It required considerable effort on Franz's part not to shout and call Rotzko, who would have heard and recognized his voice. But the shout might reach the donjon, and before the police had scaled the wall Rodolphe de Gortz would have had time to put his device in action and escape by way of the tunnel.

Franz succeeded in restraining himself and moved away from the loophole. Crossing the casemate, he went out at the other door and continued along the gallery.

Five hundred yards farther on he arrived at the foot of a staircase which rose in the thickness of the walls.

Had he, then, at last arrived at the donjon, in the centre of the place of arms? It seemed so.

But this staircase might not be the principal one giving access to the different floors. It was composed of a series of circular steps, arranged like the thread of a screw, within a dark, narrow cage.

Franz went up quietly, listening but hearing nothing, and after twenty steps reached a landing.

There a door opened on to the terrace which surrounded the donjon at the height of the first floor.

Franz glided along this terrace, and, taking care to keep in shelter behind the parapet, looked out over the Orgall plateau

Several men were still on the edge of the fir-wood, and there was no sign of their coming nearer the castle.

Resolved to meet the baron before he fled through the tunnel, Franz went round the terrace, and reached another door where the staircase resumed its upward course.

He put his foot on the first step, rested both his hands against the wall, and began to ascend.

All was silent.

The room on the first floor was not inhabited.

Franz hurried on up to the landings which gave access to the higher floors.

When he reached the third landing his foot found no further steps. There the staircase ended at the highest floor of the donjon, that which was crowned by the crenellated parapet from which formerly floated the standard of the Barons of Gortz.

In the wall to the left of the landing there was a door which was shut.

Through the keyhole filtered a ray of light.

Franz listened and heard no sound inside the apartment.

Looking through the keyhole he could see only the left side of the room, which was in a bright light, the rest being in darkness.

Franz gently opened the door.

A spacious apartment occupied the whole of this upper floor. On its circular walls rested a panelled roof, the ribs of which met in a heavy boss in the centre. Thick tapestry with figure subjects covered the walls. Some old furniture, cupboards, sideboards, armchairs, and stools, were scattered about in artistic disorder. At the windows hung thick curtains which prevented any of the light within from shining without. On the floor was a thick woollen carpet on which no footstep made a sound.

The arrangement of the room was at least peculiar, and as he entered it Franz was struck with the contrast between its light and dark portions.

To the right of the door its end was invisible in the deep gloom.

To the left, on the contrary, was a sort of platform, the black draping of which received a powerful light, due to some apparatus of concentration so placed in front of it as to be unseen.

About twelve feet from this platform, from which it was separated by a screen about breast-high, was an ancient, long-backed armchair, which the screen kept in a half light.

Near the chair was a little table with a cloth on it, and on this was a rectangular box.

This box was about twelve or fifteen inches long and five or six wide, and the cover, encrusted with jewels, was raised, showing that it contained a metallic cylinder.

As he entered the room Franz saw that the armchair was occupied.

Its occupant did not move, but sat with his head leant against the back of the chair, his eyes closed, his right arm extended on the table, his hand resting against the box.

It was Rodolphe de Gortz.

Was it to abandon himself to sleep for a few hours that the baron desired to pass this last night on the upper floor of the donjon?

No; that could not be after what Franz had heard him say to Orfanik.

The Baron de Gortz was alone in this room, and, conformably to the orders he had received, there could be no doubt that Orfanik had already escaped along the tunnel.

And La Stilla? Had not Rodolphe de Gortz said that he would hear her for a last time in this Castle of the Carpathians before it was destroyed by the explosion? And for what other reason would he have come back to this room, where doubtless she came each evening to fascinate him with her song?

Where, then, was La Stilla?

Franz saw her not, heard her not.

After all, what did it matter, now that Rodolphe de Gortz was at his mercy? Franz restrained himself from speaking. But in his present state of excitement, would he not throw himself on this man he hated as he was hated, this man who had carried off La Stilla—La Stilla living and mad—mad for him? Would he not kill him?

Franz stole up stealthily to the armchair. He had but to make a step to seize the baron, and he had already raised his hand—

Suddenly La Stilla appeared.

Franz let his knife fall on the carpet.

La Stilla was standing on the platform in the full blaze of the light, her hair undone, her arms stretched out, supremely lovely in the white costume of Angelica in "Orlando," just as she had appeared on the bastion of the castle. Her eyes, fixed on the young count, gazed to the very depths of his soul.

It was impossible that Franz could not be seen by her, and yet she made no gesture to call him to her, she opened not her lips to speak to him. Alas! she was mad.

Franz was about to rush on to the stage, to seize her in his arms, to carry her off.

La Stilla had begun to sing. Without stirring from his chair, Baron de Gortz had leant forward to listen. In the paroxysm of ecstasy, the dilettante breathed her voice as if it were a perfume. Such as he had been at the performances in the theatres of Italy, so was he now in this room, in infinite solitude, at the summit of this donjon which towered over Transylvania!

Yes, La Stilla sang! She sang for him—only for him! It was as though a breath exhaled from her lips, which seemed to remain without a movement. But if reason had left her, at least her artist soul remained in its plenitude.

Franz also stood intoxicated with the charm of this voice he had not heard for five long years. He was absorbed in the ardent contemplation of this woman he had thought he should never see again, and who was there, alive, as if some miracle had resuscitated her before his eyes!

And the song she sang, was it not one of those which would ever make his heart-strings vibrate? Yes! It was the finale of the tragic scene in "Orlando," the finale in which the singer's heart breaks in the final phrase,—

Inamorata, mio cuore tremante Voglio morire.

This ineffable phrase. Franz followed note by note. And he said to himself that it would not be interrupted as it had been at the San Carlo Theatre! No! It would not die between La Stilla's lips as it had done at her farewell.

Franz hardly breathed. His whole life was bound up in the music.

A few measures more and it would end in all its incomparable purity.

But the voice began to fail. It seemed as though La Stilla hesitated as she repeated the words of poignant grief,—

Voglio morire.

Would she fall on this stage as she had done on the other?

She did not fall, but her song fell silent on the very same note it had done at San Carlo. She uttered a cry, and it was the same cry Franz had heard on that night.

And yet La Stilla still stood there, with her adored look, the look that awoke all the deepest feelings of the young man's heart.

Franz leapt towards her. He would carry her away from this room, away from this castle.

And he found himself face to face with the baron, who had just risen.

"Franz de Télek!" exclaimed Rodolphe de Gortz. "Franz de Télek, escaped—"

But Franz did not answer, and, running towards the stage, he cried,—

"Stilla, my dear Stilla! Here I find you—alive!"

"Alive! La Stilla alive!" exclaimed Baron de Gortz. And the ironical phrase ended in a shout of laughter in which was apparent all the fury of revenge.

"Alive!" continued Rodolphe de Gortz. "Well, then, Franz de Télek, try and take her away from me!"

Franz stretched out his arms to her, whose eyes were ardently fixed on his.

At the same instant Rodolphe stooped, picked up the knife that Franz had let fall, and rushed at the motionless figure.

Franz threw himself on him to turn away the blow with which she was threatened.

He was too late, and the knife struck her to the heart. And as the blow was given there was a crash of breaking glass, and with the fragments which flew to all parts of the room, La Stilla vanished.

Franz remained as if lifeless. He could not understand. Had he also gone mad?

And then Rodolphe de Gortz cried,—

"La Stilla again escapes, Franz de Télek! But her voice—her voice remains to me! Her voice is mine mine alone, and will never belong to another."

Franz would have thrown himself on the baron, but his strength failed him, and he fell unconscious at the foot of the stage.

Rodolphe de Gortz did not even notice the young count. He took the box from the table, he rushed from the room down to the first terrace of the donjon, and was running round it to gain the other door when there was the report of a gun.

It was Rotzko who, from the slope of the counterscarp, had just shot at the Baron de Gortz.

The baron was unhurt, but the bullet shattered the box he held in his arms.

He uttered a terrible cry.

"Her voice—her voice!" he repeated. "Her soul—La Stilla's soul—it is ruined—ruined—ruined!"

And then with his hair bristling and his hands clenched, he was seen to run along the terrace, shouting,—

"Her voice—her voice! They have taken away from me her voice! Curse them!"

And he disappeared through the door at the moment. Rotzko and Nic Deck were, without waiting for the police, striving to scale the wall.

Almost immediately a tremendous explosion shook the whole extent of Plesa. Sheaves of flame sprang to the clouds, and an avalanche of stones fell on the Vulkan road.

Bastions, curtain, donjon, chapel, were nothing but a pile of ruins scattered over the Orgall plateau.

CHAPTER XVII.

It will not have been forgotten that according to the conversation between the baron and Orfanik, the explosion should only have destroyed the castle after the departure of Rodolphe de Gortz. But at the time the explosion took place it was impossible for the baron to have had time to escape through the tunnel. In the transport of grief, in the folly of despair, unconscious of what he did, had then Rodolphe de Gortz brought on an immediate catastrophe of which he could but be the first victim? After the incomprehensible words which had escaped him when Rotzko's bullet had broken the box he carried, had he intended to bury himself beneath the ruins of the castle?

In any case it was very fortunate that the police, surprised by Rotzko's shot, were at a considerable distance when the explosion shook the ground. Only a few of them were struck by the fragments which fell over the plateau. Rotzko and the forester were alone at the base of the curtain, and it was indeed a miracle that they were not killed by the shower of stones.

The explosion had done its work when Rotzko, Nic Deck, and the police entered the enclosure over the ditch, which had been nearly filled up by the fall of the walls.

Fifty yards within the wall, at the base of the donjon, a body was found among the ruins.

It was that of Rodolphe de Gortz. A few old people of the district—among others Master Koltz—recognized him perfectly.

Rotzko and Nic Deck sought only to discover the young count. As Franz had not appeared in the time arranged with his man, it followed that he had been unable to escape from the castle.

But could Rotzko hope that he had survived, that he was not one of the victims of the catastrophe? And so he cried, and Nic Deck did not know what to do to soothe him.

However, in about half an hour the young count was found on the first floor of the donjon, beneath one of the buttresses, which had saved him from being crushed.

"My master—my poor master!"

"Count—"

Such were the first words uttered by Rotzko and Nic Deck as they bent over Franz. They believed him dead; he had only fainted.

Franz opened his eyes, but his wandering look did not seem to recognize Rotzko, nor did he hear him.

Nic Deck, who had raised the young count in his arms, spoke to him again, but he made no reply.

The last words of La Stilla's song alone escaped from his lips,— *Inamorata— voglio morire.*

Franz de Télek was mad!

CHAPTER XVIII.

As the young count had gone mad, no one would probably have ever heard an explanation of the events of which the Castle of the Carpathians had been the theatre, if it had not been for the revelations which came about in this manner:—

For four days Orfanik had waited as agreed for the baron to meet him at the town of Bistritz. But as he did not appear, he began to wonder if he had perished in the explosion. Urged as much by curiosity as anxiety, he had left the town, gone back towards Werst, and was prowling about the ruins of the castle, when he was arrested by the police, who knew him from the description given by Rotzko.

Once in the chief town of the district, in the presence of the magistrates before whom he had been taken, Orfanik made no difficulty about replying to the questions put to him in the course of the inquiry ordered into the circumstances of this catastrophe.

But it must be confessed that the sad end of the Baron de Gortz seemed in no way to affect this learned egotist and maniac, whose heart was entirely in his inventions.

In the first place, on the urgent demand of Rotzko, Orfanik stated that La Stilla was dead, really dead and such was his expression—buried, and well buried, for more than five years in the cemetery of Santo Nuovo Campo at Naples.

This statement was not the least astonishing of those provoked by this curious adventure.

If La Stilla were dead, how came it that Franz could hear her voice in the saloon of the inn, see her on the bastion, and listen to her song when he was in the crypt? And how could he have found her alive in the donjon?

The explanation of this apparently inexplicable phenomena was as follows:—

It will be remembered how deep was the baron's despair when the rumour spread that La Stilla had resolved to retire from the stage and become Countess of Télek. The artiste's admirable talent and all his dilettante gratifications would thus escape him. Then it was that Orfanik suggested that by means of the phonograph he should collect the principal airs from the operas she would appear in during her farewell performances at San Carlo. This instrument had reached a high state of perfection at this period, and Orfanik had so improved it that the human voice underwent no change, and lost none of its charm or purity.

The baron accepted Orfanik's offer. Phonographs were successively and secretly introduced into the private box at the theatre during the last weeks of the season; and in this way their cylinders received the cavatinas and romances from the operas and concerts, including the melody from "San Stefano," and the final air from "Orlando," which was interrupted by La Stilla's death.

These were the circumstances under which the baron had shut himself up in the Castle of the Carpathians, and there, each night, he listened to the music given out by the phonograph. And not only did he hear La Stilla as if he were in his box, but—and that would appear absolutely incomprehensible—he saw her as if she were alive, before his eyes.

It was a simple optical illusion.

It will be remembered that Baron de Gortz had obtained a magnificent portrait of the singer. This portrait represented her in the white costume of Angelica in "Orlando," her magnificent hair in disorder, her arms extended. By means of glasses inclined at a certain angle calculated by Orfanik, when a light was thrown on the portrait placed in front of a glass, La Stilla appeared by reflection as real as if she were alive, and in all the splendour of her beauty. It was by means of this apparatus, taken for the night to the bastion platform, that Rodolphe de Gortz had made her appear when he wished to lure Franz de Télek into the castle; and by its means the young count had seen her in the room of the donjon, while her fanatic admirer was in full enjoyment of the voice reproduced by the phonograph.

Such very briefly were the explanations given in much detail by Orfanik during his examination. And it was with infinite pride that he declared himself the author of these ingenious inventions, which he had brought to the higher pitch of perfection.

But if Orfanik had explained these phenomena, he did not explain why it was that the Baron de Gortz had not had time to escape by the tunnel on to the Vulkan road. When, however, he heard that a bullet had shattered the object Rodolphe de Gortz bore in his hands, he understood how it had happened. This box was the phonographic apparatus containing La Stilla's last song, that which the baron had wished to hear for the last time in the donjon before destroying it. With its destruction his life was destroyed, and, mad with despair, he had resolved to bury himself under the ruins of his castle.

Baron Rodolphe was buried in the graveyard at Werst with the honours due to the ancient family that ended with him.

The young Count Franz de Télek was taken by Rotzko to the Castle of Krajowa, and there he devoted himself entirely to watching over his master. Orfanik had willingly handed over the phonographs containing the other songs of La Stilla, and when Franz heard the voice of the great artiste, he seemed to listen to them and recover a little of his old intelligence, and it seemed as though his mind were struggling to revive in the memories of the unforgettable past.

In fact, a few months later he recovered his reason, and through him became known what had passed during the last night in the Castle of the Carpathians.

The marriage of the charming Miriota and Nic Deck took place during the week following the catastrophe. After receiving the benediction from the pope of the village of Vulkan, they returned to Werst, where Master Koltz had reserved for them the best room in his house.

But although these different phenomena have been explained in so natural a manner, it must not be imagined that Miriota ceased to believe in their supernatural nature. Nic Deck found reasoning in vain—so did Jonas, who had as many customers as ever at the "King Mathias"—she would not be convinced. And neither would Master Koltz, nor the shepherd Frik, nor Magister Hermod, nor the other inhabitants of Werst; and many years will elapse before they will renounce their superstitious beliefs.

Doctor Patak, who has resumed his customary swagger, is often heard to say,—

"Well, did I not tell you so? Spirits in the castle! Just as if there ever were any spirits!"

But no one listens to him, and he is invariably asked to be silent when his facetiousness exceeds due bounds.

And Magister Hermod continues to base the lessons he gives to the young folk of Werst on the study of the Transylvanian legends; and for many years yet the villagers will believe that spirits from the other world haunt the ruins of the Castle of the Carpathians.

THE END.

Made in the USA
Middletown, DE
02 February 2023